HIDING FROM LOVE

The gentleman stood silently for a moment. Then he drew on his gloves and held his hand out to Leonora.

"Come," he invited.

"Thank you, but no, sir."

His next move disarmed her. Reaching forward, he took Leonora's hand and drew her from behind the table.

Much to her consternation she felt herself yield.

There was something compelling about this man's character and tone that made her will melt away like snow in the rays of the sun!

In an instant Leonora was transported into a world she had never even dreamt of, let alone experienced.

She was in a realm of air. Held close against this stranger's breast, she was weightless and dreaming.

The music seemed to penetrate her very soul.

"Oh – this is *so* wonderful," she breathed.

The gentleman said nothing, but gazed down into her ecstatic face for a moment.

Then he clasped her more tightly to him.

Too soon, far too soon, it was over and the violins fell silent.

The gentleman in the mask stood back and bowed as the sound of applause came from the antechamber.

THE BARBARA CARTLAND PINK COLLECTION

Titles in this series

HIDING FROM LOVE

BARBARA CARTLAND

Barbaracartland.com Ltd

THE BARBARA CARTLAND PINK COLLECTION

Barbara Cartland was the most prolific bestselling author in the history of the world. She was frequently in the Guinness Book of Records for writing more books in a year than any other living author. In fact her most amazing literary feat was when her publishers asked for more Barbara Cartland romances, she doubled her output from 10 books a year to over 20 books a year, when she was 77.

She went on writing continuously at this rate for 20 years and wrote her last book at the age of 97, thus completing 400 books between the ages of 77 and 97.

Her publishers finally could not keep up with this phenomenal output, so at her death she left 160 unpublished manuscripts, something again that no other author has ever achieved.

Now the exciting news is that these 160 original unpublished Barbara Cartland books are already being published and by Barbaracartland.com exclusively on the internet, as the international web is the best possible way of reaching so many Barbara Cartland readers around the world.

The 160 books are published monthly and will be numbered in sequence.

The series is called the Pink Collection as a tribute to Barbara Cartland whose favourite colour was pink and it became very much her trademark over the years.

The Barbara Cartland Pink Collection is published only on the internet. Log on to www.barbaracartland.com to find out how you can purchase the books monthly as they are published, and take out a subscription that will ensure that all subsequent editions are delivered to you by mail order to your home.

NEW

Barbaracartland.com is proud to announce the publication of ten new Audio Books for the first time as CDs. They are favourite Barbara Cartland stories read by well-known actors and actresses and each story extends to 4 or 5 CDs. The Audio Books are as follows:

The Patient Bridegroom	The Passion and the Flower
A Challenge of Hearts	Little White Doves of Love
A Train to Love	The Prince and the Pekinese
The Unbroken Dream	A King in Love
The Cruel Count	A Sign of Love

More Audio Books will be published in the future and the above titles can be purchased by logging on to the website www.barbaracartland.com or please write to the address below.

If you do not have access to a computer, you can write for information about the Barbara Cartland Pink Collection and the Barbara Cartland Audio Books to the following address:

Barbara Cartland.com Ltd., Camfield Place,
Hatfield, Hertfordshire AL9 6JE, United Kingdom.
Telephone: +44 (0)1707 642629
Fax: +44 (0)1707 663041

THE LATE DAME BARBARA CARTLAND

Barbara Cartland who sadly died in May 2000 at the age of nearly 99 was the world's most famous romantic novelist who wrote 723 books in her lifetime with worldwide sales of over 1 billion copies and her books were translated into 36 different languages.

As well as romantic novels, she wrote historical biographies, 6 autobiographies, theatrical plays, books of advice on life, love, vitamins and cookery. She also found time to be a political speaker and television and radio personality.

She wrote her first book at the age of 21 and this was called *Jigsaw*. It became an immediate bestseller and sold 100,000 copies in hardback and was translated into 6 different languages. She wrote continuously throughout her life, writing bestsellers for an astonishing 76 years. Her books have always been immensely popular in the United States, where in 1976 her current books were at numbers 1 & 2 in the B. Dalton bestsellers list, a feat never achieved before or since by any author.

Barbara Cartland became a legend in her own lifetime and will be best remembered for her wonderful romantic novels, so loved by her millions of readers throughout the world.

Her books will always be treasured for their moral message, her pure and innocent heroines, her good looking and dashing heroes and above all her belief that the power of love is more important than anything else in everyone's life.

*"I know that if I had ever tried to hide myself from love,
I would have been caught so quickly it would have
been ridiculous!"*

Barbara Cartland

CHAPTER ONE
1892

Summer term at the fashionable Fenfold Academy for Young Ladies had ended.

All sorts of vehicles were drawn up in front of the large house, waiting to convey the girls home. It always took so long for these pampered pupils to say goodbye!

Isobel Lapaz stood at the top of the steps, drawing on her white gloves.

She was leaving Fenfold for good. Her parents in Brazil had decided that they wanted her to go to school in Rio de Janeiro and live at home.

She turned to her friend Leonora.

"Oh, Leonora, I shall miss you so much!"

"I shall miss you too, Isobel."

"You must come and visit me one day."

"I would love to, but Brazil is a long way away."

Leonora did not add that it was far too expensive a journey for her to even contemplate, but Isobel understood.

"One day it will be possible, you will see, Leonora. Until then, I will never forget you. We have had so much fun together, haven't we?"

Isobel hugged her and then ran to her carriage.

Leonora watched as the coachman helped Isobel to climb in before leaping onto his box and lashing his whip.

1

Isobel leant from the window.

"Goodbye Leonora!" she waved vigorously, though her eyes were full of tears. "Until Brazil, dear friend."

"Until Brazil!" echoed Leonora without conviction.

Although the day was warm, she gave a little shiver as Isobel's carriage bowled away along the wide driveway.

There went her best friend in the world. Who knew when they would meet again?

There was nothing for her to do now but wait for the school trap that would take her to Stroud, where she would meet the public coach to Bristol and from Bristol the family trap would convey her on the last lap home.

'Home!' murmured Leonora.

How sweetly the word once rung in her ears. Now, it carried with it a vague sense of foreboding.

Leonora's beloved Papa had died two years before and her world had seemed to fall apart.

Edward Cressy had been a hero to his daughter.

The youngest son of a minor country Squire, he had refused to enter the Church or join the Army as his father prescribed. Instead he had followed his keenest interest, which was literature and had joined a publishing firm.

To his family a book was of incomprehensibly less use in the world than a garden rake or a chamber pot so this amounted to sacrilege.

They were further outraged when Edward married Lucy, who they considered beneath his station, principally because she had once worked as a Governess.

Squire Cressy cut him out of his will and only his Aunt Doris felt a sneaking sympathy for the young man.

When Edward and Lucy had a daughter, Leonora, Aunt Doris elected to pay the child's school fees when the time came.

She had been as good as her word and at the age of ten Leonora had been enrolled at the exclusive Fenfold.

At Fenfold Leonora mixed with girls from far more wealthy families than her own and yet she was never envious.

Her parents were very happy together in the little house they called Cressy Cottage and if it had not been for her desire for a good education, Leonora would have found it unbearable to leave her family each term.

Then her father died and life was never to be the same again.

Leonora's mother was left with a small pension and a little income from an investment her husband had made.

For a while she seemed to lose the will to live and even her daughter's company brought her no solace.

Fortunately Aunt Doris, a rich widow without any children, continued to pay the fees at Fenfold.

For Leonora, school became something of a refuge from the sad memories of Cressy Cottage and she became determined to make the best possible use of her education.

She continued to enjoy Fenfold, but it was always difficult on those weekends when parents were allowed to visit and take their progeny out to tea.

Her parents rarely had enough money to come all the way from Broughton to see her, let alone to indulge her for an afternoon.

Now, of course, her Mama never came at all.

Isobel Lapaz, whose parents lived so very far away in Brazil, was the only other pupil left behind at weekends and she and Leonora became really good friends, sharing a love of books and a sense of fun.

They grew bored listening to the other girls discuss the latest fashions or aristocratic weddings and they grew particularly bored when the subject of romantic love arose.

"I shall not marry till I have seen the whole world!" declared Isobel with resolution.

"And I shall not marry till I meet a man who knows as much about books as my father!" added Leonora.

Isobel considered.

"I don't think any man is as interesting as reading or travelling," she intoned solemnly and Leonora agreed.

They preferred their own company and sometimes they felt they were better off than some of the other pupils.

Poor Clara, to have her father arrive at the school in a state of inebriation!

And poor Edith Lyford, whose father had died in a far away country and whose Guardian then embezzled all her inheritance!

Isobel and Leonora were so sorry to see Edith leave Fenfold and go to live with an impecunious cousin.

Leonora gave the girl her own volume of Byron's poems and Isobel a beautiful Japanese fan.

Edith had clutched the gifts gratefully to her breast.

"I will never forget your kindness!" she sobbed.

Leonora and Isobel regarded her with concern.

"Is there no hope – of retrieving the money?"

Edith blew her nose.

"My father's partner is soon to return to England. Maybe he will help, but I don't see how. My Guardian has just disappeared!"

"Have you met the partner yet?" asked Leonora, her head on one side. "Do you know what kind of man he is?"

"I haven't seen him since I was five years old, but I remember him as tall and handsome and so kind to me. He let me dance on his toes!"

Leonora and Isobel exchanged glances.

"Well, he sounds as if he might take good care of you now," suggested Isobel helpfully.

They often thought of Edith after she had left, but as the months passed they heard nothing from her.

Then Leonora's world became turned upside down again and all thoughts of Edith flew out of her head.

*

One day she was summoned from her art class to the Headmistress's Office.

There she was astonished to find her mother sitting on a sofa, twisting her gloves nervously in her hands.

"Mama!"

The Headmistress rose and departed from the room.

Mama patted the seat beside her.

"Come and sit here, Leonora."

Leonora did as she was bidden, noting the gravity of her mother's tone.

"I have some news for you, my dear."

"News?"

"Yes. I want you to know that, after Fenfold, your future is assured."

"What do you mean, Mama? I would hope you that haven't found a husband for me, because I – "

"Hush now, my dear. I have not found a husband for you, I have, rather, found a husband for *myself.*"

Leonora's hand flew to her mouth.

"*Mama!*"

"He is a gentleman of private means. We shall not – be rich, to be sure, but – comfortable. Yes, comfortable. And you will have the protection of a stepfather. He is a man of firm temperament and – I am quite fond of him – "

She crunched her gloves into a ball and repeated,

"Quite – fond."

Leonora at last found her breath.

"Mama, what are you thinking of? I don't want a stepfather! You are doing this for me, aren't you? And you need not. I will take care of us. I will find work when I leave Fenfold."

"Bless you, bless you, my dear," her mother's eyes filled with tears, "but that is two years away – you are only sixteen – and life is hard for me. I have to struggle so."

"Don't, Mama, don't! I cannot believe you care for this – for this man of firm temperament. You loved Papa!"

Mama wiped her eyes.

"Oh yes, I loved Papa. But he is gone. And I must be certain that you – we – are suitably provided for. You must soon move in circles where you will end up meeting a gentleman of consequence."

"I don't want someone of consequence," Leonora cried. "There will never be a man of such consequence as Papa. I shall never marry – and neither should *you*."

Mama summoned all her remaining strength.

"But I already have, Leonora. *It is done.*"

Leonora sank back in her chair.

"Done! Why did you come all this way just to say it is done!"

"I-I wanted to tell you in person. When you return home – and Mr. Schilling will be there."

"Mr. Schilling!"

The name made Leonora snort with angry derision.

"He was kind enough to pay my passage here. I am – quite fond of him. Quite fond. You will – show him all the duty of an obedient stepdaughter."

She rose sullenly to kiss her mother farewell, all too aware that opposition was now futile.

6

"If that is what you want, Mama."

"It is," stated Mama firmly.

This exchange between mother and daughter had taken place just over a month ago.

Now, as Leonora watched the school trap draw up, she brooded on letters she had received from her mother.

The small touches of wit, the delicate portrayal of social life in Broughton, had all gone and in their place was a dull outline of domestic chores and lists of improvements that her new husband was undertaking in the house.

It was as if Mr. Schilling was always looking over his wife's shoulder.

Leonora went down the steps, climbed into the trap, and then turned her head to see her trunk being hauled up behind and secured with a rope.

The driver chucked at the one old horse and the trap wheeled round.

The Headmistress and one or two of the other girls who had come out onto the steps, called out their farewells.

Gravel flew out from the horse's hooves as the trap careered through the park towards the Stroud road.

After a moment Leonora opened her reticule.

Her fingers sought and closed over a folded letter.

She drew the letter out. She read it – or rather, re-read it for the hundredth time, as if to find some secret that would propel her confidence through the coming summer.

"*Dear Leonora,*" she read again,

"*I am much looking forward to meeting you and appreciating all the fine qualities that your mother assures me that you possess. I should warn you that I am a man of temperament and expect to find among all those qualities – obedience, tact, submission.*

Submission to the will of one who is determined to take up without impunity the mantle of loving stepfather.

How loving is at this stage a matter for conjecture until I discover the true nature of the responsibility I have acquired in you. Your mother is indeed profiting under my tutelage and so I hope will you.

Your waiting stepfather,

Thomas Schilling."

Unease rose higher and higher in Leonora's breast with each invidious phrase.

*

The coach from Stroud was full and Leonora was very relieved when she and her trunk were finally let down outside the *Black Jack Inn* on the road to the Bristol docks.

The coach had arrived before schedule and the trap from home was nowhere to be seen, so Leonora sat down on her trunk to wait.

She shifted about on the trunk and began swinging her foot to and fro. She was thirsty and would have loved some lemonade, but was too shy to go into the inn.

A small group of sailors trudged by and they turned to stare at the young girl waiting by the road.

Her little hat framed her pale oval face and green eyes to perfection. Red-gold curls fluttered over her pretty brow and that swinging foot revealed such a delicate ankle!

Leonora was blissfully unaware she was the object of such avid attention.

She was just as unaware of the gaze of a gentleman who had just alighted from a barouche, until he stopped to address her,

"Señorita, might I have the pleasure of inviting you to a glass of something to quench your thirst?"

Leonora looked up, blinking.

Two brown eyes in a face so olive in complexion that he could not be an Englishman, gleamed down at her.

"Why thank you indeed, kind sir," she murmured, "but how did you know I was thirsty?"

He laughed, revealing a set of small pearly teeth.

"In this heat who would not be! Will you not come in to the inn with me? It is cooler there."

Leonora shook her head.

"I am waiting for the trap to take me home."

"A pity! Beauty and the vine go so well together!"

She blushed to a deep crimson. Her natural reserve did not often invite such easy flattery.

The gentleman lifted his hat and passed on into the inn. However he did not forget Leonora for a few minutes later a tavern boy ran out with a glass of ale.

"Yon gentleman there, Señor – de – Guarda sends you his best compliments."

Leonora took a glass of ale from him.

"Please thank Señor de – Guarda for me."

The boy ran off.

Leonora took a tiny sip and grimaced. The ale was thirst-quenching but in a bitter way and she did not like it.

Nevertheless, having no desire to cause any offense to Señor de Guarda, who might well be watching from an inn window, she continued to drink.

She could not help but wonder at his kindness.

She had not been much exposed to the company of men and was therefore innocent of the general effect of her delicate beauty on their sensibilities.

She thought him a very personable gentleman. He was exotic and flamboyant.

She put the empty glass down on the trunk and rose to stretch herself.

On the opposite side of the road, a cart piled with tarpaulin-covered crates was struggling over a rut, the cart-horses straining with foam flecking their lips.

Suddenly a carriage came rolling on at great speed and Leonora thought in alarm that it would surely run into the back of the cart.

At the last minute the carriage swerved, its wheels running into the ditch at Leonora's feet.

She caught a quick glimpse of a crest imprinted on the carriage door before she felt herself engulfed in a wash of black muddy water.

"Oh," she spluttered, stepping backwards so swiftly she almost toppled over her trunk.

Her skirt was drenched – and filthy.

The carriage stopped several yards further on and, wiping wet mud from her cheeks, Leonora was starting to stride angrily to the carriage when a tiny creature leaped yelping from its open window.

The creature ran towards Leonora.

Terrified that it would end up under the wheels of some vehicle, Leonora rushed to scoop it up.

As she lifted her head from this endeavour, she felt her bonnet slip sideways and her hairpins scatter.

She turned a flushed face towards the carriage just as the door of that vehicle opened.

A young woman dressed as a maid came tumbling out. Gathering her skirts she hurried over to Leonora.

"O, *gracias*, *gracias*, Miss – ?"

"Cressy," replied Leonora.

Out of the corner of her eye she did notice that a

figure on the point of descending from the carriage now sat suddenly back into its depths.

'I am obviously not considered of enough status to be addressed directly by someone who sports a crest on their carriage,' she thought wryly.

"Oh, Miss Cressy, thank you very much!" the maid was saying. "You have saved it!"

She gazed at the wriggling creature in her hands.

"What *is* it?" she asked.

"Is a dog, miss. A *chihuahua*."

"Cheewawah? I have never heard of it."

"Is many of them in our country. My Master – " she gestured with her head towards the carriage, "he bring her for his elderly relative."

Leonora looked again and this time noticed that the figure within was a gentleman. He was leaning forward, his two hands resting atop a silver cane.

She could not discern his actual features but she felt his eyes upon her.

Half visible though he was, there was something in the gentleman's poise, the quiet intensity of his stare, that made Leonora feel a little nervous.

Even at a distance, he exuded power and authority.

He is certainly arrogant, she thought, not troubling to get out of the carriage himself to ask if I was all right.

The maid glanced towards the carriage, seemingly uncertain. Perhaps even she had expected her Master to follow her. She shifted the burden of the dog to one arm.

"The Master," she said, "is so sorry for your dress. I think – he wants to know, is there something he can do?"

"Something he can do?" echoed Leonora, realising that by this her Master probably intended to offer her some kind of recompense – which anyway she had no intention of accepting.

"Actually there *is*. He can instruct his coachman to drive with more care and less speed!"

The maid opened her eyes wide. Before she could respond the inn boy reappeared at Leonora's elbow.

"There's a trap arrived for you, Miss Schilling."

Leonora was startled to hear herself addressed for the first time by her stepfather's name and then her brow creased as she wondered where the boy had heard it.

"The trap's in the yard, through that arch. You go on, miss, and I'll go fetch your luggage."

Leonora nodded.

"Good-bye," she said to the still gawping maid and the skinny little chiahuahua.

In the yard Leonora was looking eagerly about her.

There was Finny – dear old Finny – sitting on the familiar rickety old trap, chewing on a twig. When he saw Leonora, he jumped down with a grin.

He was so pleased to see his young Mistress, he did not seem to notice her mud-stained dress.

"Miss Leonora!" he called out, tipping the twig to his forehead in a form of salute.

"Finny! Oh, it's so good to see you."

"You climb in, miss. I'll soon have you home."

The inn boy arrived with the trunk. He set it down and then stood, passing his sleeve across his forehead.

"That trunk were heavy," he grumbled as Leonora gave him a sixpence.

Finny then lifted the trunk onto the back of the trap, lashing it in place with a length of tarred rope.

Next he leaped up and reached for the reins.

"You are leaving!" came a concerned voice.

Leonora turned to see Señor de Guarda approach.

"I must, Finny arrived late and I'm sure Mama will be worried if we don't reach home before dark."

He placed his hand on the trap's high left wheel, as if to prevent its motion.

"But I am heartbroken you should think to fly away and not say goodbye to Señor de Guarda!"

Leonora blushed, aware that Finny was listening.

"Well, I will say goodbye now, Señor de Guarda."

He seized on her outstretched hand and, instead of shaking it, raised it to his lips.

Leonora gave a nervous swallow.

"Where do you live? Can I visit you?" he asked.

Leonora looked away from his melting brown eyes.

"I – that will not be possible – things at home have changed. No doubt we will meet again by chance."

Señor de Guarda shrugged.

"I doubt it. I am here for a few weeks only. Then I go home."

Leonora did not know how to respond, so she was thankful for Finny's intervention.

"We got to be a-goin', miss. Your mother and Mr. Schilling will be wantin' supper. I know there's beef pie and rhubarb."

Señor de Guarda lifted his shoulders in exaggerated resignation.

"How can I compete with beef pie and – rhubarb?"

He stepped back and blew a kiss at Leonora.

"Farewell then, lovely creature!"

Leonora waved to him as the trap passed under the arch and her cheeks burned from Señor de Guarda's gaze.

Emerging into the sun, Finny turned back towards the main road and Leonora could not help but notice that the grand carriage with the crest was still there.

The gentleman she had glimpsed in the carriage had come out and now stood twirling his cane in his hand and speaking to his maid.

Leonora noted a tall elegant frame in a velvet cloak.

As the trap passed near the carriage, the gentleman turned and Leonora quickly looked away.

She had no wish for more scrutiny from yet another gentleman, particularly one she felt aggrieved with.

'It must be that crest,' she decided, 'and his sending the maid out like that to do his bidding. And that silly dog he had brought for his relative!'

The trap skirted the gulley full of water and turned onto the road for Broughton.

Finny's voice intruded.

"That Guarda looked like a pirate," he commented.

Leonora regarded him and then gave a giggle.

"A handsome pirate, though, Finny!"

"Oh, yes, his moustache be as oiled as a gun barrel and his teeth were like the inside of seashells. He had lace cuffs too and he liked lookin' at *you*, miss."

Leonora decided that Finny had noticed too much for comfort, so she stared out at the road.

"Did you, Finny – did you send out the inn boy to ask for a 'Miss Schilling'?"

"Yes, miss. I was told to."

"Told to? By whom?"

"Mr. Schilling. He said there was to be no more of this Cressy business."

Leonora felt hot indignation rise in her breast.

14

No more Cressy business, indeed! She would like to know whether it was obligatory under the law for her to change her name to that of her stepfather!

Finny was pondering, his eyes fixed on the horse.

"I like Cressy more, miss. Schilling is – why, it's a silly name."

"What's Mr. Schilling like, Finny?"

Finny considered.

"He eats all them prunes, miss. Prunes with mutton stew. Prunes with syrup. Prunes with roast ham. He can't abide mussels and he kills snails with hot water. He has five red handkerchiefs, I've seen 'em drying on the line.

"He knows of all them gentry – so he says – and he curses under his breath. He put me to sleep in the dried out water trough only it weren't big enough, so now I sleeps in the stable loft – "

"What? Not your old room by the scullery?"

"It be a gun room now, miss. Guns and traps and fishing rods."

"Mr. Shilling does a lot of hunting then?"

"No, miss. But he likes to 'ave those things."

Leonora turned to see the light fading on the hills.

"Finny – how does he treat my mother?"

Finny kicked the running board of the trap.

"He likes her to trim his beard," he replied at last.

Leonora fell silent. What need to ask more? She would soon discover for herself.

She next wondered how Mr. Schilling might react if she had invited Señor de Guarda to visit her. She had a feeling that he would not be welcome.

She had just as clear a feeling that the gentleman

with a title, or at least travelling in the carriage of someone with a title, would have been offered the best china.

After a couple of hours the trap turned off the main road and clipped along a small country lane bordered with hawthorn.

The village of Broughton was quiet as they drove through and the gates of Broughton Hall were wide open.

After a bend in the road as they left the village, her home appeared.

All her latent fears and apprehensions burst forth as the trap drew up and she caught sight of the sign swinging over the gatepost.

Once it had borne, spelled out in cheerful scarlet, the name of *Cressy Cottage*.

Now the same sign bore a different appellation.

Schilling House it read, and Leonora's heart sank in utter dismay.

CHAPTER TWO

Mama flung open the door to greet her daughter.

"How wonderful to have you home, dearest!"

Leonora stared at her mother in shock.

As Mrs. *Cressy* her mother had been what people would call a bonny lass with bright eyes and rosy cheeks.

As Mrs. *Schilling* she had become thin and anxious, her eyes darting hither and thither as if seeking to escape.

"Mama!" Leonora cried. "You don't look well!"

She gave a laugh of enforced gaiety.

"Nonsense, dear! I'm just a little tired – I couldn't sleep last night with excitement. Now don't stand there gawping at me! Come in to meet your – Mr. Schilling."

She obviously noted the omitted 'step-father'.

Mr. Schilling was waiting in the parlour. He stood legs apart on the hearth rug, hands folded behind his back.

Leonora's first thought as she entered the room was that he looked like a stoat.

An *angry* stoat.

It was certainly accurate that everything about Mr. Schilling suggested a character permanently on the verge of expostulation. His cheeks were enflamed, the whites of his eyes were shot with red and his very moustache seemed to bristle with suppressed rage.

"My daughter, Leonora," declared Mama proudly.

He ran his eye over Leonora and frowned.

"It appears that your daughter thinks no better of her Guardian than to approach him in such a filthy state," he muttered grimly.

Leonora flushed. She had forgotten her dirty skirt, and she was about to speak when her mother rushed in,

"The fault is entirely mine, Mr. Schilling. I was so overjoyed – at seeing Leonora home I-I failed to notice the condition of her gown."

She turned agonised eyes on Leonora.

"Whatever happened, my dear?"

Leonora, disturbed at seeing her mother rendered so anxious by Mr. Schilling's displeasure, turned and replied in a low voice.

"I was waiting for Finny by the road, Mama, when a carriage ran through a puddle and flung muddy water all over me."

"Did the carriage stop?" asked Mr. Schilling.

"Why, y-yes."

"And the fellow apologised?"

Leonora hesitated, wondering whether he meant the driver or the occupant.

"His maid did," she answered finally.

Mr. Schilling took his hands from behind his back.

"*Maid*, eh? Was he gentry, perhaps?"

Into Leonora's mind swam an instant image of the gentleman with the elegant bearing and silver cane.

"There was a crest on the side of the carriage – "

Mr. Schilling gave a smirk.

"A crest? Oh, well! You are forgiven, daughter."

Leonora flinched. She did not like him calling her 'daughter'! And why the fact that there had been a crest on the carriage should so mollify him, she could not fathom.

"I suppose you took his Lordship's card, eh?" Mr. Schilling continued.

"I wasn't offered one," replied Leonora truthfully.

"And then you didn't ask for one?" he probed with a grimace. "We've a fool here, Mrs. Schilling!"

Mama wrung her fingers together.

"Oh, not a – fool, Mr. Schilling. I am sure Leonora was just a little distrait, perhaps, by the long journey and having to deal on her own with such an incident. She has been so – sheltered from the world."

"Hmmph!" grunted Mr. Schilling, his hand roving ruminatively over his moustache.

"Sheltered is good. Sheltered is desirable!"

Leonora noticed her mother's look of alarm.

"W-what do you mean, dearest, by d-desirable?"

Mr. Schilling abandoned his moustache and ran his hand over his plump red lips instead.

"Nothing, Mrs. Schilling. Why don't you take the girl up to her room, eh? And show her the improvements while you're about it."

Mama ushered Leonora quickly from the room.

"He is really a gentleman – of such temperament," she whispered as she closed the door. "But he's done so much – to improve life for us here – as you'll see."

Following her mother silently from room to room, Leonora could not help but deduce that the improvements effected by Mr. Schilling seemed generally rather more to *his* benefit than for the benefit of his wife or stepdaughter.

The huge new leather armchair in the parlour she had already noted and now she was shown pipe racks, a gentleman's writing desk, and a marquetry footstool with a pair of gentleman's slippers tellingly on top.

Her own room, it was true, did boast new muslin curtains and a new eiderdown, but she suspected that these items originated with Mama and not her stepfather.

The room Mr. Schilling shared with his wife, on the other hand, was as well upholstered as a first class hotel.

"And look here!"

Mama threw open a door in the corner of the room.

"Mr. Schilling has paid for this new bathroom."

"Very *à la mode*," Leonora muttered as she turned back. "And what is in here?" she enquired, pointing to a polished wood chest at the foot of the bed.

"Oh, that's where Mr. Schilling keeps his money," Mama answered airily.

"Why does he not keep his money in the Bank like everyone else?"

"Oh, I'm sure he has his reasons. Now, I think you should unpack and change for supper, don't you?"

All through supper Mr. Schilling demanded silence at table. Then, his repast complete, he took up a toothpick and leaned back in his chair.

"I hear you are popular at Fenfold," he began.

Leonora was unsure of what to say. She glanced at Mama for inspiration but her head was bowed.

"I am often told so," she replied carefully.

Mr. Schilling began probing his front teeth.

"Didn't you stay with some of the other girls during the holidays, though, eh!"

Leonora wondered where this was all leading.

"I preferred to return home for the holidays," she said quietly, "and at weekends, although I was invited out, I liked to remain at school with Isobel – my closest friend."

"You never went to *her* house?"

"I would have, but it's in Brazil. She is about to go back there – for good."

Mr. Schilling grunted, as if he was mollified by this information and the toothpick went to work again.

"You are not going to be invited to some Fenfold girl's estate this summer, then?"

"I think my many rebuffs of invitations in the past make such a scenario unlikely."

"Excellent," he muttered, "because I wasn't about to invite any of them here in return!"

Leonora was baffled.

Then she frowned as she remembered Finny saying that Mr. Schilling had actually *boasted* of his acquaintance with members of the gentry. Why then should he wish to avoid the company of their daughters?

"Can't stand the chatter of young girls round me," he now mumbled, as if reading her thoughts.

Wiping the used toothpick on his napkin, he leaned across the table.

"There's one contact that I *do* want you to cultivate, however, and that is your great-aunt. Lady – what is it – Carstairs? You've visited her estate before, I daresay?"

Leonora's voice was quiet.

"My Papa took me there when I was very small, but it was only once."

Mama cleared her throat bravely.

"I've told you, my dearest. L-lady Carstairs didn't dare entertain Mr. Cressy and me. The family was so very against our marriage, you see."

"And anyway," added Leonora, "I'm not at all sure I want – "

Mr. Schilling cut her off abruptly.

"What *you* want is of no consequence. It's what *I* want! And I want you to visit her this summer."

"She g-goes away to the Continent every summer," whispered Mama.

Mr. Schilling brought his palm down on the table.

"In the autumn, then. Leonora will write and get herself, and us, invited. Have you no idea, Mrs. Schilling, of the useful contacts that can be forged at these places?"

Leonora felt a nauseous wave of disgust engulf her at this admission of his objectives, but she said nothing.

That night, alone in bed, she found herself vowing never, never to make the kind of mistake her mother had made in choosing Mr. Schilling as a husband.

'Are there many men like him?' she wondered.

Her Papa had been so kind, so strong, so handsome. *He* had never made Mama unhappy.

She snuggled herself down under the quilt.

'What kind of a husband would a man like Señor de Guarda make,' she mused sleepily.

He had charm, for sure, and good looks, though not what she was used to and he was considerate, for knowing she was thirsty he had sent her out a glass of ale.

Remembering the ale, Leonora's mouth seemed to flood again with its bitter taste.

Accompanying that came an image that exuded its own bitter flavour – that mysterious gentleman with the silver cane, who had not deigned to approach her himself to apologise for his coachman's erratic driving!

He might have been an Earl or a Lord, but he was not worth a hair of her late father's head!

Yet she found herself dwelling on the image of his long elegant frame as he had stood outside the carriage in conversation with his maid – as she and Finny approached in the trap, he had turned. Might he have raised his hat to her if she had not looked away so quickly? What kind of face might she have glimpsed?

Arrogant doubtless, haughty, in all probability, but distinguished, surely, for even at a distance he had betrayed an air of authority.

The crest, a silver cane, an Earl or a Lord – these images repeated themselves in her mind until she fell into a deep if rather troubled sleep and then dreamed not of Señor de Guarda or the mystery gentleman, but Mr. Schilling!

*

It was a great relief to Leonora the next morning to discover that Mr. Schilling seemed as happy to avoid her company as she was to avoid his.

He was invariably away for days at a time, staying overnight in Bristol, from where he apparently conducted all his business.

Although Mama was vague as to the nature of this business, she did reveal that before each of his departures, he withdrew a wad of money from his wooden chest.

Leonora did not really care what Mr. Schilling did as long she was undisturbed in enjoying Mama's company.

They would relax from the moment the door closed behind Mr. Schilling, whether he was gone for just one day or three.

Gradually their old camaraderie returned, yet Mama would never complain about her husband and Leonora just supposed that Mama was reluctant to burden her daughter with her disappointments.

*

One afternoon the Rector of the local Parish called and over tea he explained the purpose of his visit.

Lady Broughton had decided to host a masked ball at Broughton Hall in just a week's time and tickets would be issued with the proceeds going to charity.

Mama, anticipating an invitation from the Rector to buy a ticket for Leonora, commented that if Mr. Schilling would not pay, then she would find the money herself.

Leonora noticed the Rector's embarrassment.

He coughed and murmured that he had not come to encourage Leonora to attend the ball, but to ask her if she would help at a lemonade stall outside the grand ballroom.

Leonora felt crushed that she was thus considered in the light of a volunteer worker and not a participant.

However, conceding to herself that it was all in a good cause, she swallowed her disappointment and agreed.

Mama knew her daughter too well to be unaware of what this acceptance cost her and after the Rector departed, she tried to commiserate with her.

"It pains me not to be able to tell these people that you yourself are the granddaughter of a Squire and as good as any of them!"

Leonora, however, laughed it all off brightly.

"Just consider it, Mama, I can be a part of the fun without going to the expense of a ball gown!"

In this Mr. Schilling, when he returned from Bristol later that week, seemed for once to be in accord with his stepdaughter.

"That's capital! She'll be seen by all the eligible bachelors of the County and it won't cost me a penny!"

Mama sighed.

"Eligible bachelors will be looking for – ladies with more eligible pockets!"

"Nonsense!" chortled Mr. Schilling. "She's a damn

good-looker, and," he added a little mysteriously, "she has her own prospects."

Mama was too grateful at his good spirits to try to discover what just he meant by 'prospects'.

*

The good spirits, alas, were quickly dispersed.

The following morning, a letter was brought in for Mama over breakfast.

Its creamy paper was bordered in black ink and she took it up with a trembling hand –

The letter came from Aunt Doris's Solicitor, who wished to inform Mrs. Schilling that the old lady had died. Since she had made no provision for Leonora in her will, the fees for Fenfold would no longer be forthcoming.

"Let me see it!" cried Mr. Schilling, snatching the letter from his wife's hand.

Leonora stared down at her plate. It was a serious blow for her, but she considered herself lucky to have had such a good education thus far, but she felt saddened by the loss of her dear aunt.

"Poor Aunt Doris," she murmured.

"*Poor*! *Poor*!"

Features contorted with fury, Mr. Schilling looked up from reading the letter.

"It's *you* who are poor, miss. Forever!"

He crushed the letter and flung it into the grate.

"Not a penny from the old witch. Not a penny."

"Mr. Schilling!"

Mama was shocked, but he then rounded on her.

"D'you think I married you out of *charity*, woman? I thought that old cow favoured your daughter! And then –

nothing! A curse on you both! This is what comes of not – cultivating your relatives!"

Understanding her husband's allusions to Leonora's 'prospects', Mama felt a chill gathering at her heart.

Leonora meanwhile listened in horror.

She had disliked him from the first moment she laid eyes on him, but she had at least supposed he did harbour some genuine affection for her mother.

Now she strongly suspected that he had married the widowed Mrs. Cressy for reasons other than affection and had expected his stepdaughter to come into an inheritance with the death of her wealthy aunt.

He had clearly believed that, although Aunt Doris had a nephew she had long ago named as heir, she would nevertheless leave a part of her fortune to the niece whose education she had paid all these years!

Leonora was left in no doubt that Mr. Schilling had intended for that fortune to end up in his own pocket.

She flinched as he leapt angrily to his feet.

"Ugly old miser!" he cried, kicking his chair with as much violence as if it was Aunt Doris herself.

Mama put her face into her hands as Leonora rose, knocking back her own chair.

"Mr. Schilling, you are upsetting my mother," she exclaimed, barely able to control the loathing in her voice.

Her tone proved a check. Mr. Schilling paused in his rant and his eyes seemed to burn in their sockets as he stared at his stepdaughter.

"Upsetting her, am I?" he muttered at last. "Well, let her reflect on this. If that withered old crone of an aunt of yours couldn't be troubled to secure your futures, then why should *I*?"

With that, he turned on his heels and slammed the door hard behind him.

Leonora put her arm around her mother's shoulder. The two of them listened, as they could hear Mr. Schilling outside, yelling at Finny to saddle his horse.

They stood barely breathing until at last the sound of hooves faded on the village road and then Leonora sank back down into her chair and looked at her mother.

"Please don't say anything," muttered Mama. "I've made my bed and now I must lie in it – but how *bitterly*, oh, how bitterly!"

"I – wasn't going to say anything, Mama," Leonora lied, seeing her mother's distraught features. "Except – to ask whether you had a pen and inkwell here. I should write a letter of condolence."

With visible relief Mama produced the items that Leonora had requested.

"You are going to write to – er – Arthur?"

"Yes, Mama."

Arthur was the nephew who had been made the sole heir of Aunt Doris's great fortune and as she had only ever mentioned him as 'young Arthur, the son of my husband's sister', Mama and she did not know his full name.

"You are not too disappointed, Leonora – about not being remembered in your aunt's will?"

"I'm most grateful that she paid my school fees for as long as she did and I wish to express that gratitude to – to Arthur, and to offer him our condolences."

"I'm not sure that he knew his aunt well. I heard he lived abroad, but you are certainly doing the right thing."

When she finished the letter, Leonora read it aloud to Mama, who expressed satisfaction with its sentiments.

Though Leonora had accepted the fact that she was

not in her Aunt Doris's will, she was nevertheless deeply saddened that she would not be able to return to Fenfold.

However Mama soon reassured her.

"Since I have remarried, I no longer need to use the income from your father's small investment. I can sell the bond and use the money to pay your fees."

"Oh, Mama!"

Leonora hugged her mother tightly.

Life suddenly seemed promising again. The only shadow was the knowledge that she would be leaving her mother to the mercy of Mr. Schilling for the school terms.

*

The following day she had other matters to occupy her, as this was the date set for the ball.

Finny drove Leonora over to Broughton Hall where they were shown round to the servants' quarters.

In the cavernous kitchen, she was handed a starched apron and was then led to the antechamber of the ballroom by a haughty butler, who gestured towards a trestle table overlaid with a white cloth.

Glasses and pitchers of lemonade stood ready.

"That's your post, miss," intoned the butler.

Leonora looked around her.

Two maids stood to attention nearby and catching Leonora's glance, they bobbed a curtsy.

"We're to fetch more lemonade when it's needed, miss. You just ring that bell there."

Leonora noticed a little handbell on the table.

The antechamber, lit by low candlelight, was dim. Through the open double doors opposite, however, she had an unobstructed view of the glittering ballroom with all its crystal chandeliers and its large vases of white flowers.

The orchestra was now striking up.

The guests were now arriving and Leonora admired their lavish costumes and ingenious masks.

One couple struck her as they waltzed by.

The lady in red velvet and wearing a gold feathered mask she recognised as Lady Broughton's daughter Maud.

The gentleman she could not place, but there was something about him that seemed vaguely familiar. It was impossible to even guess at his identity for his black mask concealed his features completely.

Soon Leonora had no time to speculate and she lost count of how many glasses of lemonade she served or how many times she rang the handbell for fresh pitchers.

At last supper was announced and the tide of thirsty revellers began to change course for the food-laden tables in the Great Hall at the other end of the ballroom.

Leonora took the opportunity to stack up the used glasses on the trays provided and the maids hurried over to take the trays down to the pantry.

She retied her apron and began to smooth back her tousled hair.

"You must be much in need of a drop of lemonade yourself," came a voice at close quarters.

Leonora looked up.

The lady in the gold feathered mask was standing in the door and her imperious tone betrayed her to be exactly who Leonora had guessed – Maud Broughton.

"Thanks very much. I've already had two glasses," said Leonora, her eyes straying to Maud's companion, the gentleman in the black mask.

He was removing his gloves with his head bowed, but he looked up sharply at the sound of Leonora's voice.

Through the mask, his eyes met hers and blushing, she averted his penetrating gaze.

"I've danced every dance so far," Maud declared, "and I'm *parched* – I must have a glass of lemonade."

Leonora poured one for her.

She stopped and then offered one to her companion.

The gentleman shook his head gently, his eyes still fixed on Leonora.

"Oh, *he* would rather have champagne, I'm sure!" laughed Maud.

"I want nothing," he declared in a low voice.

Maud glanced at him and then stiffened slightly as she noted his intense focus on Leonora.

She turned round and, raising her glass to her lips, surveyed Leonora over its rim.

"Do you like dancing?" she asked sweetly.

"Yes, I do" responded Leonora.

"Rather a shame, then, to be tucked away into this corner all evening, isn't it?"

Her voice betrayed a note of false commiseration.

"Well, at least I can *watch* it all," replied Leonora.

"Oh that's just not good enough!" exclaimed Maud as she clicked her fingers at the orchestra.

"Violinists, could you strike up please!"

Leonora saw the violinists glance at each other and then lift their violins to their chins.

"There," crowed Maud as the first strains of a waltz rose up. "Now you can dance. There's nobody here to see. They're all far too busy at supper. *Go on.*"

Leonora shrank back.

"I-I cannot – madam."

"Of course you can. My companion here will be only too happy to partner you. Won't you?" she added, turning almost fiercely on the gentleman in the black mask.

The gentleman stood silently for a moment. Then he drew on his gloves and held his hand out to Leonora.

"Come," he invited.

Leonora's jaw clenched.

She guessed that Maud wished to humiliate her in some way and she was determined not to allow it.

"Thank you, but no, sir."

His next move disarmed her. Reaching forward, he took Leonora's hand and drew her from behind the table.

"Come," he repeated.

Much to her consternation she felt herself yield.

There was something compelling about this man's character and tone that made her will melt away like snow in the rays of the sun!

"Splendid!" hissed Maud through gritted teeth as the two passed her and entered the ballroom.

"M-my apron," whispered Leonora unhappily. "I cannot dance in an apron!"

In response her partner reached out behind her and deftly untied the apron strings.

In an instant Leonora was transported into a world she had never even dreamt of, let alone experienced.

She was in a realm of air. Held close against this stranger's breast, she was weightless and dreaming.

The music seemed to penetrate her very soul.

"Oh – this is *so* wonderful," she breathed.

The gentleman said nothing, but gazed down into her ecstatic face for a moment.

Then he clasped her more tightly to him.

Too soon, far too soon, it was over and the violins fell silent.

The gentleman in the mask stood back and bowed as the sound of applause came from the antechamber.

"Bravo!" cried Maud Broughton in withering tones.

"Your apron," she hooted, holding out the article to Leonora. "You will have to revert to being a servant again, I'm afraid, after that taste of the high life!"

Leonora thought that she heard the gentleman draw in his breath, but she could not be sure.

She took the apron with fingers that trembled a bit.

"I am afraid that you are under a misapprehension," she said in a low voice to Maud. "I am no servant. I am here because the Rector asked me to volunteer my services for which," she added more coolly, "I am not being paid."

Maud toyed with the sleeve of her dress.

"Well, I suppose I must apologise. Not a servant, eh? So who are you? What is your name?"

"Leonora Cressy."

Maud pursed her lips.

"The daughter of the widowed Mrs. Cressy? Then isn't your name now – Schilling?"

Leonora tossed her head.

"I suppose my name is what I choose it to be!"

Maud gave a dry laugh.

"I interpret that answer as meaning you don't care to be known as Mr. Schilling's daughter? Well, who could blame you? His manners – or lack of them – have attracted a good deal of unfavourable comment already. He must be a trial to live with."

Leonora was stunned.

She was well aware of the gentleman listening. She wondered why he, who had treated her with such gallantry a moment ago, should now permit his friend to address her with such effrontery.

With a degree of bitterness she thought of the adage that '*birds of a feather stick together*'.

Maud and her companion were both aristocrats and would close ranks against someone considered an outsider – even though that outsider's own grandfather was at least a Squire who had owned a large estate of his own.

"Whatever the merits of Mr. Schilling may be," she said now with conviction, "he is my stepfather and I do not take kindly to your describing him in that manner."

Maud seemed unabashed.

"A flash of claws!" she sighed, almost approvingly.

Leonora might have responded even more fiercely, but that at this moment a footman passed with a sconce of fresh candles, all burning brightly with their light falling on her and illuminating her features.

"Good Heavens!" exclaimed Maud. "What a little beauty we have here!"

Leonora was totally taken aback by this unexpected change of subject, she had no idea of the alluring spectacle she presented.

Her eyes gleamed like emeralds.

Her skin, so milky and translucent by nature, was, after the exertions of dancing, flushed deeply with redness, resembling a lovely pink rose after rain, as her golden curls tumbled loosely about her brow.

"Quite exquisite," added Maud with an obvious but grudging admiration.

She turned to her companion.

"Don't you agree?"

Leonora could not help but glance at her erstwhile dancing partner, who had remained so silent.

She was immediately struck by his attitude. It was as if he had not only been watching and listening intently, but had also been – deliberating.

His gaze which she believed with a sudden rush of pleasure had never left her face, he now allowed to fall.

"Exquisite indeed," he agreed in a bored manner.

Leonora's sudden feeling of elation at his interest in her faltered, particularly as Maud seemed so satisfied with the tone of his reply.

"Well, come along now," she said, taking hold of his arm and leading him away. "I'm absolutely starving."

Leonora watched them depart. Then she put on her apron again and resolutely tightened its strings.

For a few delicious moments she had tasted what the girls at Fenfold had discussed so ardently – *romance.*

She had experienced its highs and lows within the space of less than twenty minutes and she had survived – though whether unscathed was another matter.

It would be so difficult to forget the strength of the arm that had encircled her waist and the breast to which she had been so firmly grasped.

The maids brought more pitchers of lemonade and the orchestra resumed as guests began to stream back from the supper tables.

Leonora was soon busy filling up the glasses once again and she tried not to watch the couples dancing.

Several times out of the corner of her eye, she felt that she saw Maud Broughton swirl by, but not always in the arms of the gentleman with the black mask.

Towards ten o'clock she took a glass of lemonade

for herself and wandered to the window. It overlooked the sweeping driveway at the front of the house.

A carriage waited outside, its steps set down and its door open with a footman standing to one side.

Light streamed out onto the gravel as the front door opened. Leonora's heart skipped two beats as a figure in a black mask strode elegantly down the steps and, gesturing to the coachman, climbed into the carriage.

The footman then slammed the carriage door.

'*The crest*!' she thought. 'It is surely the same as the one I had espied on the carriage that had splashed my dress by the *Black Jack Inn*!'

Which meant that the gentleman she had thought so arrogant then was the very same as the masked stranger in whose arms she had swooned this evening!

She rubbed the glass with the edge of her apron and pressed her face more closely to the pane, but the carriage was already turning.

She could not see the crest now, but she *could* make out a figure at the window.

As she watched, this figure seemed to look her way.

Too far to make out any features, it was yet near enough for her to see the gloved hand that waved in tender farewell!

Entranced, she intently watched the carriage move away under the elms that lined the drive.

In a moment, carriage, crest and passenger were all swallowed up in darkness.

CHAPTER THREE

For the next few days Leonora found herself in an unfamiliar state.

At the sound of horses' hooves on the road beyond the cottage her heart would begin to beat quickly.

When passing Broughton Hall on her way to see the baker or butcher, she could not refrain from stopping and peering through the gates in the ridiculous hope of seeing *that* carriage bowling towards her.

When the postman arrived she could not help flying down the stairs two steps at a time as if one of the letters might be from *him*!

After all, he did know her name, but it would not be so difficult to find out where she lived.

He had held her close in the dance – closer she was certain than was usual in these affairs – closer than she had seen him hold Maud Broughton.

She had even heard him agree with Maud that she, Leonora, was indeed exquisite.

Admittedly he had indicated a certain boredom with the subject, but might that not have been to deceive Maud? Because later he had waved to her as he had departed.

Was it really beyond the realms of possibility that he would come for her?

Time and the continued silence on the part of the mystery gentleman soon disabused Leonora of this conceit and after a few days she was forced to concede that he had all but vanished into thin air.

'You are just a silly fool, Leonora,' she told herself severely as she brushed her hair one morning.

'Perhaps you *are* pretty – in an ordinary way – but there are so many pretty women in the world. So why on earth should a gentleman choose one in an apron, hot and bothered after serving endless glasses of lemonade!'

Resolving now that the object of her affections had merely been amusing himself at her expense when he was waving from his carriage, she determined to put the whole incident at Broughton Hall out of her mind.

For this reason she refused an invitation from Maud to attend a tea party to thank all the volunteers.

What Maud construed from her refusal she would never know, as shortly Maud departed on a visit abroad to some exotic islands in the Atlantic apparently.

All this time Mr. Schilling remained in Bristol or London – exactly where, neither Leonora nor Mama cared.

*

One morning a dray cart lumbered to a halt outside the cottage and a man jumped out and began to haul down packages.

Mama, who had seen the cart arrive and gone out to investigate, called out excitedly to Leonora.

"Do come down. These packages are for you."

Leonora descended the stairs in puzzlement as the packages were carried into the living room.

"They are from Bristol," sighed Mama, reading the labels. "They must be from your stepfather."

As the wrapping paper was removed and the boxes opened, Leonora's astonishment knew no bounds.

Here were dresses and gloves and stoles of a quality she had never in her life possessed.

She could never imagine Mr. Schilling capable of such taste and Mama's hands were at her cheeks in awe.

"Can that be *ermine*? Whatever is Mr. Schilling thinking of! He must have such plans for you, darling!"

Leonora dropped a white fur wrap back into its box.

"That's what worries me, Mama."

Finny carried the boxes up to Leonora's room and offered to help put their contents in chests and wardrobes.

"You'll look a Princess in this, miss" he marvelled, holding up a beautiful lavender silk gown.

Leonora took the gown, trying not to reflect on that night at Broughton Hall – if only she had been wearing this dress when she danced with the masked gentleman!

Mr. Schilling arrived two days after the packages and he was in such obvious jovial spirits that Leonora and Mama were almost suspicious.

"Did some parcels arrive?" he quizzed Leonora as he took off his brown mantle in the hall.

"Thank you – yes," replied Leonora, twisting a blue handkerchief in her hot fingers. "I must admit to being – astonished. Did you choose the contents yourself, sir?"

To her surprise, Mr. Schilling deliberately ignored her question.

"What's for supper?" he asked, turning to Mama.

"Mutton stew and baked prunes, but Mr. Schilling, Leonora wishes to discuss the generous gifts you sent her."

"Later, later!" he puffed.

All through supper, whenever Leonora glanced Mr. Schilling's way, he would give her a conspiratorial wink.

She was at a loss as to what this might portend.

After supper she, Mama and Mr. Schilling repaired to the parlour, where he sank into his leather chair whilst Leonora sat on a stool by Mama's chair.

He brought out his pipe, caught her eye and gave yet another of his winks.

"No more worries about *your* future!" he muttered.

Leonora straightened up on her stool.

"I don't consider my future a worry. I shall return to Fenfold and continue with my education. When I leave I hope to find employment as a Governess."

Mr. Schilling lit his pipe.

"You can forget about Fenfold. I'm not paying for you to return there."

"I don't expect you to. Mama has kindly offered to pay the fees."

"Oh, has she?"

Mr. Schilling took a deep draw on his pipe and let out a trail of smoke before replying,

"And where, pray, will she find the money?"

Mama stared at him.

"Why, I have been saving up the dividend from my late husband's bond. So there's a small amount there and I shall now sell the bond and capitalise on its full value."

Mr. Schilling gave a strange smile.

"Can't sell what you don't have," he remarked.

"D-don't have?"

Mr. Schilling pointed his pipe at her.

"It's just like this, you see. Once a woman marries, what's hers is her husband's. Surely you know that?"

"The issue n-never arose b-between us – "

Leonora was watching Mr. Schilling.

"Why don't you get to the point, sir?"

He took another puff on his pipe.

"I took the liberty of selling that bond, as was my right," he responded with ill-concealed relish.

"I spent so much renovating this cottage, I needed some funds to invest in new investments. And so there you have it, Mrs. Schilling. You no longer have any money, so Leonora can't go back to school and there's an end of it."

"H-how could you do t-this to me – to us?" Mama dropped her head to her breast and began to weep silently.

Leonora felt as if the breath had been knocked out of her body.

She had guessed that her stepfather was a fortune-hunter as well as an opportunist – but that he also more or less amounted to a thief was too much to bear.

She took her mother's hand in hers.

"Don't cry. It'll work out for the best, I'm sure."

Mr. Schilling laughed and waved his pipe at her.

"And that's where you're correct for once, missy. You can tell your mother that there's no need to take on so. Not when she's got a fortune sitting right here at her knee."

Leonora's fingers tightened on Mama's hand, while she looked up slowly and fearfully.

"W-what do you – mean, Mr. Schilling?"

"I mean just this, Mrs. Schilling. Those clothes that were sent to your daughter have a purpose. They're for her entrance into Society."

Leonora could not believe her ears.

"Do you mean that *I* am the 'investment' you have spent my mother's money on?"

"Sending you to Fenfold was an investment, wasn't it? Well, I reckon I've found a better one, though for your information, the money for those clothes didn't come out of my purse – or your mothers. I had some other projects I wanted to invest in."

Leonora and her mother stared at him blankly.

"Then just who – who paid for the clothes?" asked Mama in a low voice.

Mr. Schilling leaned back in his chair and surveyed his wife and stepdaughter with satisfaction.

"Her *fiancé* did," he replied.

Leonora paled.

"My f-fiancé? I haven't got a *fiancé*!"

"You have now! And he's as rich as Croesus!"

"Explain yourself," demanded Mama.

"Yes," echoed Leonora. "Explain yourself – sir."

"With great pleasure, ladies. One of my colleagues in Bristol invited me to his Club for a game of cards.

"We'd just taken a refreshment break when I was approached by a certain Lord Merton. He has been living abroad for some years, but he recently returned to England to find himself a young wife. He knew about my pretty stepdaughter and thought she was the ideal candidate."

"But – this Lord Merton has never even seen me!" cried Leonora in utter bewilderment.

"Oh, yes, indeed he has," returned her stepfather in a triumphant tone. "Twice! Once when his carriage ran through a puddle and splashed your gown and once when you were helping out at Broughton Hall."

Leonora's head swam.

The masked gentleman!

She had surely wished he might come for her, but could she ever have imagined that it would be in such an underhand way – to approach her stepfather over a game of cards in an inferior gentleman's Club that reeked of stale tobacco smoke and dirty ale glasses!

"I would have pressed for good terms, of course," continued Mr. Schilling. "But since he offered me a very lucrative business deal if I brokered the match, I shook on it there and then."

Leonora gasped loudly, her disillusion complete.

"You and he – *shook* on it? As if I was a horse or a mule or a bale of hay?"

Mama gave a low moan.

"You have sold her, Mr. Schilling! *Sold her*!"

He looked surly.

"Now don't you two give me trouble about it. I've done the best that could be done for Leonora. How else is she going to get a husband of worth?"

Leonora leapt up passionately from her stool.

"I do not consider a man who *barters* for a wife to be a man of worth!" she cried. "I don't consider any man *you* choose for me to be a man of worth!"

The mask was stripped from her gentleman's face and what she saw in her mind's eye was an expression as greedy, cynical and immoral as her stepfather himself.

Mr. Schilling spluttered and rose to his feet.

"What else is there for you, eh? Being a skivvy at the big house, invited to put on an apron and wash dishes? You fouled up your relationship with your aunt and ended up left out of her will. You're not going to foul up this arrangement. You're going to do what's good for you and, more to the point, what's good for *me*!"

"I would rather die than marry a man I could not love," cried Leonora. "And there's one thing I'm sure of. I could never never love a man of *your* choosing."

"Why you, you ungrateful little madam!" he roared. "You'll do as I say or you both can go to the dogs."

Mama from her chair caught at his arm.

"P-please, Mr. Schilling, d-don't threaten so."

He threw off her hand and brought his face so close to Leonora's that she could smell the tobacco on his breath.

"I agreed with Lord Merton that you'll marry him next week and that's what you're going to do."

Leonora lifted her chin defiantly.

"*Never*! Never!"

Mr. Schilling was provoked by this beyond control and lips drawn in a snarl, he raised his hand as if to strike Leonora across her cheek.

Before any blow could fall, Mama rose with a cry from her chair.

"Mr. Schilling! This I cannot permit. Lay a finger on my daughter – and I shall – order you from my house."

Mr. Schilling rounded on his wife in fury.

"*Your* house? You forget. You're married to me so it's *my* house now. Obstruct me and it's *you* who will be ordered out!"

Blood drained from Mama's face. She staggered back and fell in a dead faint to the floor.

*

Leonora scrutinised the doctor's face anxiously as he emerged from her mother's room.

"H-how is she?" she asked fearfully.

The doctor hesitated.

"Miss Cressy, your mother's heart is weakened, she needs peace, rest and freedom from strife of any kind."

"I see," mumbled Leonora faintly.

43

The doctor patted her arm kindly.

"So you see, it is up to you and your stepfather to help her recover."

Leonora bit her tongue from replying.

She was convinced that it was the strain of being married to Mr. Schilling that had made her mother ill in the first place. It was not *possible* for her to recover under his ministrations.

Not that Leonora harboured any illusions as to the likelihood of Mr. Schilling helping to nurse his wife. He had shown so little concern except to mutter complaints at now being saddled with an invalid as well as a fool.

And he had not relinquished his determination to make Leonora marry Lord Merton.

Leonora watched the doctor descend the stairs and then turned and went in to her mother.

Mama's eyes fluttered open as Leonora approached the bed and she noticed that her mother's cheeks were wet.

"God, Leonora. I am so so sorry."

"Sorry, Mama?"

"If I had not married that man." Mama began to grow agitated. "I thought to better our situation but I – "

"Hush, Mama, hush."

Leonora knelt down by the bed and reached for her mother's hand. At her touch, Mama grew calm. Her eyes closed again and she slept.

She needed to get her away from Schilling House.

But how? Aunt Doris might have offered sanctuary but she was dead and her nephew by marriage had not even troubled to reply to Leonora's letter of condolence.

Even after she had tiptoed away quietly to her own room, Leonora still wrestled with the problem.

If only she could talk to Isobel, the one friend in the world she could divulge her plight to, but Isobel was now far away in Brazil.

She had only recently received a letter from her.

Isobel had written that a wealthy family in Rio were seeking an English governess. If only, she added wistfully, Leonora could take up the employment.

Leonora sighed as Brazil was the other side of the world and she feared that she would never see Isobel again.

She climbed into bed and lay staring at the ceiling.

She knew that this time was when she was at her most vulnerable. This was when the image of the masked gentleman and the memory of how it had felt to be in his arms would come to torment her.

Since she had discovered his true nature, however, she felt even more determined to dispel him from her mind.

*

During the next couple of days Leonora contrived to keep out of Mr. Schilling's way. She spent much of her time at her mother's bedside, wracking her brains as to how she might affect her Mama's escape.

It was Mama herself who came up with the answer.

In a melancholy mood, she now asked Leonora to go through her personal possessions.

"In case I – do not recover," she explained.

"Don't be silly, of course you are going to recover."

Mama persisted,

"My jewellery is in that box. I don't want it to be appropriated by anyone else. I want you to take them now and hide them. There is a lovely ruby ring that was given to me by my dear friend Phyllis."

Leonora gave a start.

Phyllis. Of course!

"Mama," she ventured. "Do you happen to know where Phyllis is now?"

"I think she is living somewhere in Norfolk, on the coast, I have heard."

"*Where* on the coast?" persisted Leonora.

Mama looked troubled.

"Well, my dear, I-I don't rightly know. She was brought up in Cromer. She might have returned there."

Leonora thought this was as good a guess as any.

Later that day, she sat down to compose a letter to Phyllis Godwin, care of the Post Office, Cromer. Someone at the Post Office may know of her, surely?

She had just sealed the envelope and sent Finny off to post it in the village when she heard the sound of hooves on the road beyond her window.

Thinking it might be the doctor calling in to see her mother, she hurried to greet him.

She stopped in her tracks at the top of the stairs. In the absence of Finny, Mr. Schilling had answered the door.

"Lord Merton, what a pleasure!" she heard him say.

She sank down and peered through the banisters.

She could make out a tall figure in a green velvet coat turned away from her, his head slightly inclined as he conversed with Mr. Schilling.

It was he – *her masked gentleman*!

She gazed down at his head and her lip curled.

Some of his hair was *grey*!

She frowned to herself. Not only was Lord Merton importunate and presumptuous, he was also obviously far too old for her. He must be *at least* thirty!

She slipped back to her mother's room.

When Mr. Schilling appeared as she knew he would and invited her in whispered tones to come to the parlour to meet a visitor, she refused.

She said she well knew who the visitor was and she had nothing of any interest to say to him. Besides, she was unable to leave her mother's side while she was so ill – as a gentleman like Lord Merton would surely understand!

Outmanoeuvred, Mr. Schilling withdrew in a huff and shortly Leonora heard Lord Merton mount his horse and ride away. She would not let herself go to the window to watch his departure.

When Finny returned he reported that a fellow on a horse had lifted his hat to him as he passed by.

"Did you see the gentleman's face, then?"

Finny shook his head.

"Not really, miss. I was thinkin' I liked his hat."

Leonora gave a shrug. What did it matter? She did not care what Lord Merton looked like anyway.

*

A reply arrived from Cromer.

Phyllis wrote that she would be only too delighted to offer Mama refuge. Sadly she could not extend hospitality to Leonora as well as the house she lived in was too small.

"No, Leonora," Mama stipulated firmly, "I am not going without you. I just cannot leave you to the mercy of your stepfather."

Leonora had to think quickly. It was not her nature to lie, but she was convinced that this was a matter of life and death. She *had* to get her mother away.

"You must not worry about me, Mama. I've – just received a letter inviting me to stay with – with my friend Isobel's aunt."

"You have?"

She drew out Isobel's letter and waved it under her mother's nose.

Mama wavered.

"Well, I'm sure it's very kind of this aunt, you must give me the address so I can write and thank her."

"You are not to worry, Mama. Isobel's aunt is now on her way to her estate in – in Wiltshire. She will send a carriage for me and as soon as I arrive I'll write to you and – give you the address."

Mama sank back on her pillows sleepily.

"Well, if you promise to do that, dear, then I shall be able to go to Cromer with a light heart."

Feeling relieved Leonora tiptoed from the room.

She was making a list of what she should pack for her mother's journey when Mr. Schilling appeared.

"Lord Merton is calling after tea," he growled. "I don't want any excuses from you – you are to come down and be civil to your future husband. And I want you to wear one of those gowns he sent you."

Leonora's face set like stone, but she said nothing.

When Lord Merton did arrive for tea, he summoned Leonora by means of the brass handbell on the hall table.

Leonora regarded herself in the mirror with grim satisfaction before leaving her room.

She had not donned one of the gowns sent to her by Lord Merton, as to have done so would, she believed, have signalled her acquiescence to his unwelcome suit.

Instead she put on one of her oldest and shabbiest skirts with an ugly patched blouse and she did not trouble to arrange her hair either.

She walked swiftly to the stairs and stared down.

Lord Merton was below.

The light was behind him and he carried such a big bouquet of flowers that his face was barely visible.

Mr. Schilling was nowhere to be seen – obviously leaving the field clear to Lord Merton to exert his charms.

"Good afternoon, Lord Merton," she began. "My stepfather advised me that you intended to pay a visit. All I have to say is this – I do not wish to entertain you. I bear you no ill will, nor do I have any interest in you as a suitor.

"Though I *do* find it astonishing that you persist in attempting to see me when you know full well that my dear mother – the only one in the world who may demand my devoted attention – remains indisposed."

Without waiting for a reply, Leonora turned on her heels and fled to her mother's room.

A few minutes later Mr. Schilling burst in.

He was carrying the bouquet and his furious face seemed yet another scarlet bloom amidst the many.

"How dare you," he spluttered, vainly attempting to keep his voice low. "You have insulted Lord Merton."

"I have merely made my position perfectly clear."

"You are not entitled to any position," he hissed.

He threw the bouquet onto the chest at the foot of the bed and pointed at it.

"Those were for your mother. Tell her when she awakes. You can also tell her that her daughter is confined to the house until she obeys my demands."

He then stormed from the room, barely preventing himself from slamming the door.

It was a half hour or so before Leonora heard the front door open, indicating that Lord Merton was leaving. She moved to the window and looked out, just in time to see him mount his horse and ride away.

She had to admit that his bearing was manly though his features remained as unknown to her as ever.

When Finny returned from his daily errands in the village, Mr. Schilling sent him up with a letter for Leonora.

The letter was from Lord Merton.

"*I am sorry that you misunderstood the meaning of my visit today. I only came to enquire after your mother's health and bring her some flowers. I would hope that she will recover soon.*

Meanwhile I look forward to the time when you will feel more disposed to see me."

'That will be *never*,' thought Leonora scornfully, crushing the letter in her grip. 'I will *never* ever agree to the wishes of my odious stepfather – a man who has made my darling Mama so unhappy!'

*

Two days later Mama left for Norfolk.

Leonora remained cheerful, helping with all the last minute preparations.

Then as she and Finny half carried Mama down the stairs, Mr. Schilling looked on with a disgruntled air from the parlour window.

Leonora waved her goodbye brightly, but even as the trap disappeared along the road, her mind was racing.

She had told Mama that she was leaving the next day too and she felt that she somehow had to make that little white lie come true.

Though utterly relieved that her mother would gain respite from the tensions of Schilling House, she was only too aware that she herself was now left unprotected from the machinations of her stepfather.

Who knew what he would do to attain his goal?

She soon found out the answer to that question.

Tidying up Mama's room, she was suddenly made alert by the sound of a key turning in the lock behind her.

Spinning round, she raced to the door and shook the handle.

Too late!

Sensing somehow that Leonora intended to fly the coop, Mr. Schilling had decided to take no chances.

She was now a prisoner at Schilling House!

CHAPTER FOUR

"Finny! Finny!"

Finny put down the pail of water he was taking to the horse and listened. He was *sure* he had heard someone softly calling his name.

"Finny! Up here."

He lifted his head and blinked as he saw Leonora leaning out from a bedroom window.

"Miss Leonora!" he called out in loud surprise.

"Sssh." Leonora put a finger to her lips.

She mouthed her next few words.

"Is – is Mr. Schilling around?"

"No, miss, he ain't and I thought the house empty – till I sees you."

"Is the horse still in harness?"

"Yes. I was just takin' him some water."

"Good. Give him some oats as well and while he is eating, fill the trap with hay from the stable."

"Fill the trap with hay?"

"Yes, then bring it here beneath the window."

Finny shook his head, wondering if Miss Leonora had not gone a little mad.

"But – what are you goin' to do, when I brings the trap round?"

"I'm going to jump out of the window, Finny, into

the trap. So make sure there's plenty of hay to cushion my fall! I am depending on you."

Finny picked up the pail, grumbling.

"I'll do it. But it's beyond me why you don't use them stairs."

"Oh, Finny!"

Leonora, amused despite herself, drew her head in from the window.

Finny had been away for two days and had no idea of what had transpired in his absence.

It had been two days of hunger and humiliation for Leonora. Two days when her odious stepfather wheedled and finally threatened her from outside the door.

He threatened her with starvation if she would not agree to marry Lord Merton and as she continued to refuse, even Mr. Schilling grew alarmed.

Last night in her sleep, she had been half aware of the sound of a key turning, the door opening and closing –

This morning she had awoken to find a tray on the floor with a jug of water and two slices of bread and jam.

It had tasted like a breakfast fit for a King and as she was eating, Leonora had formulated her plans.

The only person in the whole world who could help her escape was Finny and she prayed that Mr. Schilling would go off on one of his many mysterious errands.

Leonora was becoming convinced that he gambled, which would explain his need for large sums, such as her mother told her he extracted weekly from his chest.

She crossed to the bed, where a sheet lay open over the quilt and began to throw onto it the few items she had chosen for her flight.

She was not in her own room and had of necessity been forced to ransack her mother's wardrobe.

Leonora stepped back and took one last look at the room. She seized her mother's hairbrush, then extracted two necklaces from her jewellery box.

She closed the lid and thought. Then she picked up the box and carried it through to the bathroom, where she hid it in an aperture she had noticed near the rafters.

At least Mr. Schilling would not get his hands on it!

She returned to the bedroom and surveyed the sheet with satisfaction before knotting its four corners together to form a makeshift bag.

She hauled it to the window and hoisted it on to the window seat. Then she turned and went to the chest at the foot of the bed.

She rapidly found what she was seeking – a brown leather pouch with the letter '*F*' embroidered onto it. Why '*F*' and not '*S*' for Schilling she had no idea.

The pouch contained close on fifty pounds.

She weighed it on her palm and then tucked it into her reticule.

She knew her action would be construed as theft, but she refused to feel guilty. As far as she was concerned, this sum of money represented the sum that Mr. Schilling had stolen when he sold her mother's investment bond.

There was a whistle from outside the window and Leonora ran over and leaned out.

Finny waited proudly below. The trap beside him was drawn up under the window, its passenger box packed high with golden hay.

"Finny, you are an angel," whispered Leonora.

Lifting her bundle, she threw it down onto the hay.

She tightened the strings of her reticule round her wrist and then clambered out onto the sill herself.

Finny covered his eyes with his hands.

She swallowed, took a deep breath and pushed off.

She landed very safely in the middle of the hay and began to laugh elatedly as Finny rushed across.

"I've escaped, Finny, I've escaped."

"Escaped?"

"Escaped from Mr. Schilling. He locked me in my mother's room. I've been there for two days."

Finny's eyes were as round as full moons.

"Locked you in? Two days?"

"Finny, stop repeating everything, please. There is no time to be lost."

She looked round her anxiously, half expecting Mr. Schilling to appear at any minute.

"I must get away."

"I'm comin' too," insisted Finny quickly.

"Finny – I do need you to drive me to Bristol. But you'll have to leave me there and bring the trap back."

Finny's lip trembled a bit, but he said nothing and began to brush wisps of hay from the passenger seat.

Leonora waved him away.

"No, leave it. I'll ride beside you on the driver's seat. You don't want Mr. Schilling to see hay on the path."

"Don't want to come back at all if there's only Mr. Schilling here. He locked you in, I don't like him. I'll beat him with an egg whisk!"

"I rather hope you do, Finny, except I don't want you to get into trouble on my account. But come on – it would be dreadful if he caught me now."

Finny tied Leonora's bundle securely to the back of the trap, then leaped into the coachman's seat.

The poor old horse, who ten minutes ago had been dreaming of the shade of his stable, found himself setting out again on a long journey.

Finny set him almost at a gallop.

They went the long way round, avoiding the village and taking side roads, encountering no one until they came out onto the Bristol road, where they fell in with a flow of coaches, hay carts and lone riders on jaded steeds.

Leonora clutched her reticule, her mind afire.

Her mother would be shocked to hear that she had run away and she must write to tell her she was safe.

She would have to admit that she had told a white lie, but she hoped Mama would understand that it had been for a serious purpose.

She would also have to admit to her mother that she had taken Mr. Schilling's money and explain why.

Finny broke in on Leonora's thoughts.

"Why you goin' to Bristol, miss? Why aren't you goin' Norfolk way, where your mother be?"

Leonora wondered how much she should tell Finny.

"There's no room where my mother's going," she replied at last, "and anyway I want to go somewhere where I can work and pay back anything I have borrowed – "

Finny looked concerned.

"If you need more, miss, I've got five shillings."

Leonora looked at him gravely.

"Thank you, Finny. I shall not need it, however. I have enough for my – immediate purposes."

"And what's that, miss?"

"I intend to find a ship at Bristol that is sailing for Brazil," she replied. "I'm going to visit my friend Isobel."

Finny looked alarmed.

"Cross an ocean, what's full of whales and water? What would you want to do that for, miss? Why?"

"Because I don't want to marry Lord Merton – "

"But any girl would want to marry a Lord!"

Leonora turned and regarded him.

"Have you ever seen Lord Merton, Finny?"

"I've seen his horse, though, tied to the gate when Lord Merton a-came visitin'."

"Well, let me tell you, Finny, I'd rather marry the horse. It's not so *old* and *grizzled* as its Master!"

Finny was too astounded at her admission that she would rather marry a horse than a real live Lord to say any more on the subject.

*

It was late in the afternoon when the trap reached the gates of Bristol Docks and Leonora looked about with interest as they drove through.

She directed Finny towards a long low building that she surmised correctly was the Ticket Office.

Finny waited in the trap while she went in.

The Office was nearly empty and behind the door a gentleman sat reading a newspaper, but her gaze was fixed nervously on the clerk behind the counter.

Leonora coughed and he regarded the young lady in front of him and he glanced beyond her as if expecting to see a chaperone of some sort.

"I was wondering – whether I could book passage on a ship – " began Leonora.

The clerk looked over the top of his glasses.

"Did you have any particular ship in mind, miss?"

"Well, any ship going to Brazil would do."

"Brazil, eh? Are you travelling alone, miss?"

"I am," admitted Leonora, colouring.

"What age are you?"

Leonora lifted her chin defiantly.

"Old enough to travel, sir! I am sixteen."

The clerk seemed to consider.

"There's a ship embarking for South America this evening," he said at last.

"That's wonderful!"

"It's a cargo ship, miss. It takes passengers, but I should warn you that there's no First Class."

"Oh, that is quite all right with me," said Leonora, secretly grateful that she would not be put in the position of having to reveal that she could not afford First Class.

She must conserve her small funds, since she had no idea how far they would stretch before she could secure employment at her destination.

The clerk picked up a pen to write out a ticket.

"Do you have much luggage, miss?"

"N-not much," confessed Leonora, thinking of the sheet knotted at its four corners.

"And I presume your papers are in order?"

"My p-papers?"

"Your travelling papers, miss."

It was something Leonora had not considered – had not even thought necessary. She stared in utter dismay at the clerk, as he slowly raised his head to look at her.

"*Your papers*," he repeated.

"I-I am afraid I-I quite forgot them – in the rush of packing. Are they – essential?"

The clerk regarded her severely.

"Miss, you cannot leave this country or enter into another country without them."

Leonora, in complete despair at seeing her plans so unexpectedly dashed, burst into unrestrained tears.

"You don't understand," she sobbed. "I-I must go to Brazil. There's nowhere else for me now."

She was aware of a slight rustle behind her as the gentleman by the door folded his paper and rose to his feet.

"I think I may well be of some assistance," came his strangely familiar voice.

Leonora swung round, her eyes opening wide as she recognised the face before her.

It was that of Señor de Guarda!

*

The clerk regarded Señor de Guarda with interest.

"And how might you be of assistance?" he asked.

Before replying to him, Señor de Guarda took out a handkerchief and handed it to Leonora.

As he intended, she pressed it to her brimming eyes and so did not notice his next move, which was to take his wallet from his pocket and move closer to the counter.

"I might be of assistance to the tune of five pounds, for example," he murmured pointedly.

The clerk ran his tongue over his lips and glanced at Leonora, who was still dabbing the tears away.

"I'm assuming the five pounds would require a few – um – stipulations to be overlooked?"

"Exactly. So what do you say?"

The clerk lowered his voice.

"I take it – you know this young lady, sir?"

Señor de Guarda shrugged.

"Certainly I do. You may be assured."

"Well then, sir!" The clerk reached out and swiftly drew the five pound note from Señor de Guarda's hand. "I shall issue a ticket immediately."

Leonora raised her head to Señor de Guarda.

"He is – selling me a ticket?"

"Of course. All you must do is pay for it."

He stepped aside as Leonora rested her reticule on the counter and with trembling fingers she took from it the leather pouch embroidered with the letter '*F*'.

Señor de Guarda's eyes settled on this for an instant before he looked away, whistling softly under his breath.

The clerk took Leonora's money and then held up her ticket in an admonishing manner.

"When you reach Brazil, miss, you'd better tell the authorities there that you mislaid your papers on the ship. Or I'll be in trouble for letting you aboard at this end."

"I'll do just what you say," agreed Leonora, eagerly taking her ticket.

"*The Teresa of the Sea* sails at eight o'clock sharp," continued the clerk, replacing his glasses on his nose.

Leonora, ticket clutched to her breast along with the pouch and the handkerchief, turned to Señor de Guarda.

"How can I ever thank you, Señor?"

"You can thank me by being an amiable companion on the long voyage," he smiled.

"You are on *The Teresa of the Sea* as well?"

"I am," he replied, opening the Ticket Office door and ushering her through.

Finny leaped down from the trap outside.

"You was a long while, miss," said Finny, throwing a strange glare at Señor de Guarda.

Leonora explained that there had been a problem.

"Which this gentleman kindly solved for me. You remember Señor de Guarda from the *Black Jack Inn*?"

"I remember him," mumbled Finny curtly.

He pointed at the leather pouch, which Leonora still clutched to her breast.

"What you doing with the Master's purse? He'll be cross if that's gone."

Leonora flushed crimson.

She quickly tucked the pouch back into her reticule, and as she did so, the handkerchief that Señor de Guarda had given her fluttered from her grasp.

"Oh, I'm very sorry. You were so kind to lend it to me. I am ashamed to say I was in sore need of it."

"Don't be ashamed, my dear lady," smiled Señor de Guarda, picking it up. "Your tears were most charming."

Leonora noticed that his gaze strayed to her reticule as if musing on its contents.

"You have been most kind," she repeated, uneasily thrusting the reticule behind her back.

"Just how could I not come to the aid of a damsel – how do you say it – in distress? Fleeing her cruel father, perhaps – or an unwanted suitor?"

She gasped in alarm and he put a finger to his lips.

"I say nothing – *nothing*. Now you must excuse me while I go and collect my luggage from the hotel. We shall meet on board later. At supper perhaps?"

Leonora nodded mutely as he walked away.

"He's a-going over the ocean too?" asked Finny.

"Yes," said Leonora, realising that she was not as pleased at this prospect as she had been a few minutes ago.

He had guessed too near to the truth for her liking.

Finny was scowling.

"I don't like this, miss, come back home with me."

Leonora shuddered.

"I can't, Finny. Please don't ask again. Just help me find the ship and then – you must leave and drive back to Broughton."

Sullenly Finny helped her up beside him.

They drove around the docks until they located *The Teresa of the Sea*, a solid if undistinguished vessel,

Her hold was open and great lengths of steel were being lowered into its depths.

Leonora stepped down from the trap and started up the gangplank with Finny following her, the knotted sheet slung over his shoulder.

The gangplank swaying beneath her feet reminded her that she had never been on a long sea voyage before and she wondered if she would be seasick.

An Officer greeted her on deck and took her ticket. He examined it closely and then pointed aft.

Finny made to move but the Officer barred his way.

"You can go no further unless you are travelling."

Leonora turned. Faced with the moment of truth, she was stricken at having to bid farewell to her last friend, her last link with home and childhood.

"Oh, Finny, I shall miss you so!"

"You oughtn't to go," he muttered.

"I must, I must! But let me embrace you!"

Finny stood stiff as Leonora threw her arms around him and then he turned round and made his way miserably down the gangplank.

On the quay he turned again and stared up at her.

She had to fight back an urge to run after him.

Then she hoisted up the sheet– too embarrassed to ask any of the porters to carry such strange luggage for her – and made for the cabin indicated on her ticket.

She threw off her hat and looked around.

The cabin was rather small but comfortable enough. There was a washstand with a bowl and jug, towels laid out and a writing table with a stool.

On the table was a pen, inkwell and writing paper.

Leonora clapped her hands to her head – she had intended to write to Mama while the ship was still in port. She should not have dismissed Finny but asked him to wait so that he could post the letter for her onshore.

She rushed to the porthole and peered out.

Her cabin was portside and she could see the quay, but there was no sign of Finny.

Well, she must write the letter anyway, there would surely be a Steward who would take the letter ashore and post it before the ship sailed.

She sat at the writing table and took up the pen.

"Darling Mama," she wrote,

"By the time you read this I shall be far away, but you are not to worry about me, please.

I am quite safe, on board The Teresa of the Sea *and sailing to Brazil. My friend Isobel will look after me when I arrive. I am going to work as a Governess.*

When I have earned enough to pay for your fare, I will then send for you. I am sure you understand why I had to lie to you and why I have run away.

Please do not return to that dreadful Mr. Schilling and please do not tell him where I am.

I took his money, Mama, to pay my fare. He will tell

you that I am a thief, but I intend to pay it back when I can – after all he stole your money without compunction.

As for Lord Merton – if you should encounter him tell him nothing either. Except to take away those clothes he bought for me!

Your loving Leonora."

She reread the letter, folded and sealed it, picked up her reticule and then stepped out into the corridor.

She peered at cabin doors as she hurried along, but most were closed, although one or two stood open.

In one a startled young girl looked up as she passed, catching a glimpse of a long bony face and pale hair.

"Desiree!" a voice called from inside the cabin and the girl turned away.

On deck the Officer who had taken Leonora's ticket agreed to send someone ashore with her letter.

"There is plenty of time," he added. "We don't sail for another three hours."

Leonora returned to her cabin where she untied the sheet and stared down at what it had held.

Her mother's dresses suddenly appeared to be old-fashioned and somewhat large.

She held them up against her with a sinking heart. She would need a needle and thread to take them in or she would be a laughing stock on board.

She sank onto the bed, a green dress in her hands.

She remembered this dress. Her mother had worn it years ago on the occasion of their one and only meeting at a hotel with Aunt Doris.

She recalled the elderly lady smelling of lavender water gazing down at her solemnly.

Even then Aunt Doris had talked affectionately of

her sister's son, Arthur, her sole heir, and described him as a handsome lad with a streak of wildness.

She lay back on the bed, holding the dress tightly as if this vestige of her mother and happier times might prove of consolation in the trials that surely lay ahead.

She closed her eyes, aware of the slight movement of the ship as it lay at anchor and then sleep overtook her wearied senses.

A strange sound woke her.

She thought it was the bellow of a bull. Then she realised it was the ship's funnel!

She sat up and from the porthole she could see the quayside receding.

She must have slept for nearly three hours!

The ship was sailing and all of a sudden her recent resolution and courage deserted her.

She stumbled over to the porthole, aware already of a slight sickening rise and fall beneath her feet.

Lights were flickering onshore in the gloom.

England was passing.

Home was passing away. Mama, Finny, Fenfold – all were slipping away beyond the glass – all vanishing, perhaps *forever*.

And that night – that wonderful night when she had danced with the masked gentleman – before she knew his character, before she knew his name.

Tears welled and spilled onto her cheeks. Leaning her forehead on the glass, Leonora began to weep.

She was so alone and the ocean ahead was so vast, so fearful to her.

Whatever had she been thinking about, to set out on such a journey?

Even marriage to the arrogant Lord Merton might have been preferable to this immense loneliness!

No, she rebuked herself sternly. Lord Merton had bartered for her like a farmer at a fair.

He had sought to buy her affections with beautiful dresses and ermine. He had seen her twice and decided that he could possess her, as easily as snapping his fingers.

He had frequented the same disreputable Club as her stepfather and had bribed him for access to her.

How could she ever yield her heart to such a man!

A sudden tap at the cabin door made her start and she turned, drying her tears.

"C-come in," she called wondering who it could be.

She hoped it was not Señor de Guarda!

The door opened slowly and a solitary figure sidled in, balancing a loaded tea tray.

Leonora started with a cry of amazement.

How was it possible?

There before her stood Finny!

Finny, dressed as a cabin boy and beaming at her for all he was worth.

CHAPTER FIVE

Over steaming cups of scented tea and shortbread biscuits, Finny related his story.

He had only got as far as the gates to the dock when a wheel on the trap had come loose.

As he was struggling to tighten the wheel a carriage pulled up quickly and the passenger – a gentleman – had offered the help of his driver.

While the driver attended to the carriage wheel, the gentleman drew Finny into conversation.

He wondered why Finny looked so sad, and Finny divulged that it was because he had to return to cheerless Schilling House, whilst the Mistress he had served so long sailed off to Brazil without him.

The gentleman had looked very thoughtful at this.

Leonora was alarmed.

"Oh, Finny! Suppose he was an Officer of the law, sent after me by Mr. Schilling?"

Finny guffawed.

"I knowed he wasn't, miss, because his boots were too good! And he was kind into the bargain. Besides, I didn't give him your name. I just said 'Schilling House'."

The gentleman had said it would be an easy matter to arrange to have the trap returned to Schilling House on Finny's behalf. Meanwhile, he was sure that he could pull enough strings to get Finny a job on board the ship bound for Brazil, if he so wished.

"And he did," added Finny proudly. "I'm cabin boy to all the private cabins."

Leonora shook her head wonderingly. Who could this gentleman be, who had such influence that he could secure employment for someone who had never even set foot on a ship before, let alone worked on one!

When she asked the gentleman's name, however, Finny shuffled his feet and frowned.

He said he could not quite remember, but Leonora had the distinct impression that he had been specifically requested to forget!

Well, whoever this kind benefactor was, she was delighted to have Finny with her.

He departed for his new duties, so Leonora finished her tea and started hanging up her mother's dresses.

When the supper gong sounded, she was forced to think carefully about what she would wear for this, her first appearance in public.

She chose the same green dress she had mused over earlier. She put it on and pulled a face before the narrow pier glass. The sleeves were too long, the hem trailed and the material ballooned about her slender waist.

What was she to do?

She seized on the idea of using the red ribbon of her own dress to tie about her as a sash and she was then able to tuck the dress into this and so shorten the length.

The gong sounded again as she quickly twisted up her hair and wound it about her head.

Pinching her cheeks to give herself a little colour, she opened the door and stepped out into the passage.

She almost immediately collided with the figure of a gentleman emerging from the cabin opposite.

They both apologised and he stood aside to allow Leonora to pass.

Feeling rather self-conscious about her unorthodox appearance, she could not meet his eye, but muttered her thanks to the top of his smart blue waistcoat.

This done, she made to move on, only to trip almost at once on the hem of her dress. Flustered, she stopped, feeling even more of a fool than before.

"Please go on," she asked the gentleman. "I must attend to my skirt."

"Arthur Chandos at your service," came the polite rejoinder. "Perhaps I could be of some assistance?"

There was nothing for it now, she had to look up.

The face that gazed down at her was of a mien that she might have deemed to be haughty but for an expression of genuine concern.

As she thus regarded Mr. Arthur Chandos, a strange metamorphosis came over him.

The concern of his gaze faded, replaced by a look she could not quite fathom.

His pupils flared as he followed the line of her lips, the outline of her soft cheek, the halo of her golden hair.

It was as if he was devouring her every feature.

Leonora felt most uncomfortable under this intense scrutiny and yet she could not turn her face away.

"M-Mr. Chandos?" she ventured.

At the sound of her voice he half-closed his eyes as if to dispel a tormenting image and passed his hand across his brow.

"I am sorry that I seem a little distracted," he said. "You remind me of someone very dear."

To her great surprise, Leonora found herself almost

jealous of this 'someone', whose remembered image alone was capable of arousing such fervour.

'*Will I ever inspire such passion*?' she wondered.

The supper gong rang again loudly.

Mr. Chandos hesitated, obviously remembering his previous offer of assistance to Leonora.

"You may leave me, Mr. Chandos," she said with a wry smile. "I can manage my dress – alone."

He appeared almost relieved, bowed and went off down the passageway.

Leonora could not help staring after him. She now realised that something about his figure – something about the tone of his voice had disturbed her from the beginning.

She felt as if they held out an echo of happier times, but why this should be so she could not say as she most certainly had never met anyone called Mr. Chandos before.

Suddenly she did not want to lose sight of him, so tucking the top of her skirt tightly under the sash around her waist, she hurried in his wake.

Catching up with Mr. Chandos, she slowed to walk just a few feet behind, but he did not look back once.

She noticed that he cut a figure of some distinction and the crew and Officers greeted him with deference as he passed and, when he reached the entrance to the salon, the Steward at the door inclined his head respectfully.

'Yet he is not a Lord or a Duke or anything like that,' thought Leonora. 'He's just a plain Mr.!'

In the salon he made his way to the Captain's table and she noted that the Captain rose to greet him.

Suddenly uncertain, she looked around. There were three other tables in the salon other than the Captain's.

Where should she sit?

A waiter approached and indicated a place for her.

Three people were already seated at the table – one middle aged couple and a girl of about Leonora's age, who she recognised as the girl with the pale lanky hair she had glimpsed through an open cabin door.

The couple looked askance at Leonora's attire, but proffered the usual pleasantries, introducing themselves as Mr. and Mrs. Griddle and the girl as their daughter Desiree.

The name seemed so unlikely for the thin miserable creature who bore it that Leonora was a little bemused.

Desiree did not look up, but sat staring down at the tablecloth as Leonora introduced herself and said she was pleased to make their acquaintance.

She was relieved to have her back to the Captain's table, as she was not sure that she would have been able to prevent her gaze lingering on the enigmatic Mr. Chandos.

Mrs. Griddle, on whose ample bosom hung a man's watch and chain, announced brightly that she knew all the other passengers' names already.

"There aren't that many of us on board," she began with an air of disdain. "Mr. Griddle booked on this vessel, but I should have much preferred a passenger ship myself!"

Mr. Griddle, a lean, angular gentleman with sparse brown whiskers, looked suitably apologetic.

Mrs. Griddle then pointed out at an adjoining table an elderly man with white hair seated next to a woman of Hispanic features. Two gaunt young men sat with them.

"The old man is a music professor," she whispered. "Travelling with his wife and sons."

Leonora hesitated and then turned her head towards the Captain's table.

"And what do you know of – that gentleman over there?" she asked somewhat shyly.

"Him? He's a Mr. Chandos, rather too haughty for his own good. Came on board on a whim.

"I saw him. Walked right up the gangplank without a stick of luggage. But he must be of note, because he was shown without delay to one of the very best cabins!"

'*Opposite mine*,' thought Leonora, wondering into which category of cabin that put her own. She had surely not paid for one of the best?

"Why he should be travelling now on a cargo vessel when he is a man of wealth I don't know," continued Mrs. Griddle. "But a man of wealth he is – look at the quality of his attire. I do know a thing or two about fashion."

Mr. Griddle leaned across to her.

"My wife worked for a tailor and I owned a small shop in Fetter Lane. We are going to São Paulo to open a new hosiery shop."

Leonora imagined their trunks full of silk stockings and boned corsets and gentlemen's gaiters.

"And your daughter is to be an assistant?"

"My daughter will be what I tell her to be," growled Mrs. Griddle.

Leonora was taken aback at her vehemence. She glanced towards Desiree, who had at last raised her head.

The girl's air of doleful resignation was painful to behold and for a moment she forgot all about Mr. Chandos.

The next moment there was a general stir as Señor de Guarda appeared, wearing a flowing scarlet cravat and his fine moustache shone with oil. There was no doubt that he was a striking figure.

His beady eyes were quickly roving the salon and when they settled on Leonora, he made his way over to her with a smile indicating a complicity that she shrank from.

"Miss Cressy," he murmured. "You are looking – if I may so – charmingly unique."

Mrs. Griddle now looked at Leonora with renewed interest. That he should acknowledge this young woman at all obviously impressed the indomitable matron.

"Are you – acquainted with Señor de Guarda?" she asked Leonora.

"A – little."

He threw back his head.

"A little? Why, dear Mrs. Griddle, we are nearly old friends – Miss Cressy and I. I can safely say I know more about her than anyone here."

Leonora protested weakly as he put his head on one side.

"You are my discovery, Miss Cressy. I claim you. Particularly as I know we are one of a kind."

Though not in the least understanding him, Leonora wished that he would not be quite so revealing before the curious gaze of the Griddles.

"Señor de Guarda has been – most helpful to me in helping to secure my passage," she admitted in a low voice to the Griddles, attempting to explain what must seem an unlikely connection.

Señor de Guarda grunted with pleasure and pulled out the chair next to her.

Mrs. Griddle leaned across to Leonora.

"Señor de Guarda is in corsets," she said grandly.

Leonora blinked.

"I beg your pardon?"

"He is a large supplier of whalebone to the hosiery trade. He used to supply our shop in Fetter Lane."

Señor de Guarda gave a wave of his hand.

73

"And this time I arrive in London to find that you and Mr. Griddle on the point of leaving."

Leonora turned to look at Señor de Guarda. He was certainly a colourful character, and she supposed it was not that unnatural she should have found him appealing when she first encountered him outside the *Black Jack Inn*.

"Would anyone object if I joined this table?"

Leonora's head snapped up.

Through a dim mist she discerned the approach of the gentleman who had so much intrigued her earlier – Mr. Chandos, who, according to Mrs. Griddle, had boarded *The Teresa of the Sea* on a mere whim!

Leonora looked to Mrs. Griddle, expecting her to invite Mr. Chandos to sit down, but it was Señor de Guarda who replied and in an unexpected fashion –

"We are a little crowded already, I think."

Leonora suppressed a loud exclamation of surprise at this unexpected discourtesy.

Mr. Chandos seemed unperturbed, leaning on the back of a vacant chair regarding Señor de Guarda coolly.

"Indeed? Is another person expected?"

He looked awkwardly at the vacant chair.

"Well – no."

"Perhaps you are unaware, then, that this is a table for six?" enquired Mr. Chandos dryly.

"Perhaps – " muttered Señor de Guarda.

The two men locked eyes.

It was paramount that someone break the impasse and invite Mr. Chandos to be seated.

Leonora was trying to summon up the courage to speak when she was amazed to hear Desiree's timid but determined voice.

"P-please do join us, Mr. Chandos. I'm sure Mama and Papa will be as h-happy as me to have your company."

Turning to look at her, his features softened.

"I shall be delighted to sit by such a gracious young lady," he cooed.

Leonora found herself surprisingly indignant.

It was not fair! She had been just on the point of issuing the self same invitation! Now Mr. Chandos would never know that she was as gracious as Desiree Griddle!

Señor de Guarda, outmanoeuvred, sat down with a sniff of disgust and unfolded his napkin.

"We were a pretty little party until *he* arrived," he whispered in Leonora's ear. "He is trouble."

"Oh, you are undoubtedly misinformed as to Mr. Chandos's character," she whispered back urgently. "I can assure you he is a gentleman."

He drew back and regarded her with narrowed eyes.

"You are acquainted with him?"

"Not – really."

"Then how can you tell? For my part, I think no gentleman travels without luggage."

Leonora said no more on the subject, but turned to observe the rest of the table.

Mr. Chandos had taken his seat and Mrs. Griddle, put to shame by her daughter, was hastening to make up for her previous lack of good manners.

"Of course we are most honoured that a gentleman such as yourself should choose to join our humble group," she purred at Mr. Chandos. "I've been admiring the cut of your waistcoat since you arrived. Am I right in thinking that it is a Savile Row acquisition?"

"In fact, it was made by a tailor in Rio de Janeiro."

Mrs. Griddle simpered.

"Indeed? Well, they are more advanced there than we thought."

Mr. Chandos looked amused, but was saved from the necessity of further chat on the subject of his waistcoat by the arrival of the waiter with a pot of lobster bisque.

As the waiter ladled out the soup Leonora regarded Mr. Chandos from under lowered brows.

His features in repose indicated a man of authority, a man used to giving orders. And he really was very very handsome. His jaw was firm, his lips finely wrought, his nose supremely aristocratic, whilst his brow –

Leonora broke away from this train of thought in horror as she saw that he was looking directly at her. He must have sensed her eager scrutiny!

Her colour heightened and she was relieved that the waiter's arm now interposed between herself and the object of her admiration.

"Soup, madam?" asked the waiter.

"Thank you, yes. Just a little."

She stared down as the liquid flowed into her bowl. She shook out her napkin and at last dared to sneak another glance at the intriguing Mr. Chandos.

He was no longer looking her way. Spoon in hand, his head was inclined towards Desiree, who was speaking with a degree of animation that Leonora would never have suspected her to possess!

Mr. Chandos listened intently to Desiree's chatter, only now and then interposing a rejoinder.

Leonora could see Mrs. Griddle was acutely aware of this *tête à tête*.

"Why are you scowling?" came Señor de Guarda's voice at Leonora's ear.

"Was I?"

"Yes. To see your pretty lips turned down – ugh!"

"Well, you must desist from looking at me then!"

Leonora spoke in a louder voice than she intended and there was an immediate pause around the table.

With an attempt at nonchalance, she reached to take a bread roll from the bread-basket. Seeing eyes turn and follow her movement disbelievingly, she looked down.

Her sleeve – too wide for her wrist by a good inch or two – was dangling in her soup.

"Oh," she whimpered in despair, trying not to note what she took to be Mr. Chandos's dry amusement.

Señor de Guarda beckoned the waiter over and took the white cloth from his arm and then proceeded to dab at Leonora's damp sleeve.

She looked at him for a moment and then raised her eyes towards Mr. Chandos, who was regarding the Señor's hand on her wrist with a frown.

His gaze then travelled up to Leonora's face. She drew in her breath as she saw again that same fevered glow in his eyes, that same devouring hunger.

Then it was gone and he looked away.

Mrs. Griddle shook her head across the table.

"I am so amazed, Miss Cressy, that your mother let you travel without attending first to your wardrobe."

"*Mama!*" chided Desiree.

Leonora blushed.

"My m-mother was not in a position to – attend to my needs," she tried to explain, "and I decided quite on the spur of the moment to – sail to Brazil."

Mrs. Griddle's brows furrowed inquisitively together and she gave a wag of her finger.

"Young lady – why am I now getting the distinct impression that you are some sort of *runaway*?"

"Bull's eye, eh, Miss Cressy?" whispered Señor de Guarda.

Leonora tried to ignore him.

"I am not – running away from my mother, at any rate," she emphasised truthfully.

She wanted to add that anyway none of it was Mrs. Griddle's business, but she managed to bite her tongue.

She was after all travelling alone and without the permission of her parents and thus she needed to keep such busybodies as Mrs. Griddle on her side if she could.

"You are not a runaway from school?" interposed Mr. Griddle unexpectedly.

"Oh, I should never have wished to do that," cried Leonora with some passion. "I loved my school."

"You are lucky," came in Desiree. "I *hated* mine."

Mrs. Griddle rounded on her daughter in outrage.

"Hated Gadbolt? One of the finest Academies for young ladies in England! Nonsense! I'm sure Miss Cressy would have been only too delighted to attend Gadbolt."

Her eye swivelled towards Leonora.

"Where *did* you go, dear?"

"Fenfold," replied Leonora simply.

Mrs. Griddle swallowed.

Fenfold was seen as *the* best school for daughters of the gentry, whilst Gadbolt was merely a finishing school of sorts for the middle classes.

It was unendurable that Miss Cressy should have attended a finer school than her own poor Desiree. With some degree of ill nature, she cast about for some way of reducing the stature of Fenfold,

"I hear there's been some hint of scandal attached to Fenfold. It's common knowledge that one of the pupils had to leave when her Guardian stole her Trust money!"

Mr. Chandos looked up sharply.

"The poor girl was surely not to blame for the fact that her Guardian was a scoundrel," he countered stiffly.

Leonora, remembering Edith Lyford's sobs the day she had to leave Fenfold, was gratified that he had spoken up on the innocent girl's behalf.

Mrs Griddle was unappeased.

"But for a school of that reputation to take in a girl with such questionable connections!"

Leonora now felt exasperated and spoke up,

"When Miss Lyford came to Fenfold her father was still alive and *he* was certainly not questionable! He was a businessman who worked abroad, and when he became ill he asked his London solicitors to appoint a Guardian for his daughter, and it was *they* who suggested the gentleman who turned out to be entirely untrustworthy."

"Bravo, Miss Cressy," applauded Señor de Guarda.

Mrs. Griddle sniffed.

"Nevertheless – " was all she could find to say.

Desiree, who had been listening keenly to the story of Edith, now leaned eagerly across the table.

"Whatever happened to Miss Lyford after she had to leave Fenfold?" she asked Leonora.

Leonora toyed unhappily with her napkin.

"I don't quite know. I lost touch with her. I wish I hadn't, but my own life took such an unexpected turn that I was quite taken up with other matters."

She thought for a moment.

"I do know that Edith Lyford had some hope of her father's business partner coming to her aid."

Mr. Chandos leant forward to pour a glass of wine.

"Did this partner live in England?" he asked.

"No, he – why, I believe he lived in Brazil. Yes, it's where her father had his business. Isn't that strange?"

"Strange?"

"Well, if he didn't come to England as Miss Lyford hoped he would, then he would still be in Brazil. I might run across him in Rio, and if I did, I would put Edith's case to him and insist he help her retrieve her money."

"Did you learn his name?" asked Mr. Chandos.

Leonora's face fell.

"No, I didn't. Edith never mentioned him by name. She said she had only met him once, when she was a child. She remembered him as handsome and kind and he let her dance on his toes. He sounded just the kind of man with whom – "

Leonora blushed and added,

"With whom – one might easily fall in love."

She scarcely knew why she had introduced such a subject, as it was one she and Isobel had scorned to discuss at Fenfold.

"Why, Miss Cressy," said Señor de Guarda, turning to regard her with interest. "So that is how to win your heart – dancing on my toes?"

Aware of Mr. Chandos's stony silence, she wished the earth would open and swallow her up.

Desiree meanwhile, her hands clasped tight on the table, stared at Leonora with shining eyes.

"Miss Cressy? Can you be by any chance running away *for love*?"

Leonora was spared the necessity of a reply by Mrs. Griddle, who turned and slapped Desiree's wrist.

"You are *not* to bring up such a subject, daughter!"

Desiree shrank back in her chair as a flash of anger crossed Mr. Chandos's face.

He concealed the emotion quickly, but Leonora did notice. She also noticed how from that moment on he took no further part in the general conversation, but redoubled his attentions on Desiree.

He filled her glass with wine, helped her to bread rolls, and even removed the bones from her fish when she expressed her dislike for the task.

From time to time Mrs. Griddle glanced over at her daughter and Mr. Chandos with an air of satisfaction that dismayed Leonora.

She had never considered herself a great beauty, but *surely* she was more pleasing to the eye than Desiree?

The girl had the distinct air of a shadow – a skeletal creature with hair so pale it was almost white and pupils lacking any discernible colour.

She was a mere mouse!

And yet here was the elegant and distinguished Mr. Chandos, *showering* her with attention.

It – was not – fair!

She, Leonora, had encountered him first!

CHAPTER SIX

A half hour later Leonora stood staring out over the dark waves. A sea breeze blew and she gave a shiver.

She wished that Finny would hurry with the shawl he had gone to collect from her cabin.

It was Finny who had suggested a stroll on the deck before retiring for the night.

He had found her in dismal spirits in her cabin. She had left the supper table before pudding, unable to bear any longer the sight of Desiree monopolising Mr. Chandos.

Leonora was relieved to see Finny and had agreed with alacrity to a stroll. The sight of the star-laden sky had lifted her spirits, but the night air was so cool.

Placing her hands on the ship's rail she gazed out at the horizon, a thread of pale light between sea and sky.

Shivering again, she looked for Finny.

There was no sign of him, but her eye was caught by the red glow of a cigar in the shadows.

"Hello?" she called out.

The red glow advanced.

Her heart lurched as she saw that it was held in the left hand of Mr. Chandos. He went to the rail and flicked the cigar overboard, then leaned on his elbows to watch it being swallowed by the deep.

He said not a word and she wondered unhappily if he did not feel inclined to talk to her because it was she and not Desiree.

"It's a beautifully clear night," she ventured at last.

He turned his head slightly, but she could not read his expression as the moonlight was behind him.

"It is indeed," he replied. "Had we been on deck a short while ago we might have seen the Scilly Isles. We should reach the Azores in two days time."

"You have – made this journey often, then?"

"Not often enough."

He raised his head to regard the sky and the large white moon riding there.

"An Atlantic moon," he murmured.

Leonora followed his gaze.

"Is it – so very different – from other moons?"

"Look at it. Is it the same moon you can see from your bedroom window in England?"

"Well – no. At home, at most times, it looks softer as if it's wrapped in muslin. Only on very frosty nights is it like this – sharp as a blade."

"Alas! It's not often enough that I witness a frosty English night."

"Oh, you do not live in England?"

"I live in Brazil," he answered.

"In – Rio?"

"In Rio," came the firm reply.

Recalling that the Griddles were going on to open a shop in São Paulo, she felt an ungallant surge of triumph.

Her rival Desiree would be leaving the field free!

She studied his profile as he stared out to sea.

That nose really was most aristocratic! Perhaps he *was* indeed an aristocrat – the younger son of an Earl or a Duke. After all, she really knew very little about him. In fact she really knew too little about him to feel as she did.

With a sudden rush of shame she thought of Isobel and their pact never to succumb to the allure of romance.

What had happened since parting from Isobel?

Firstly she had found Señor de Guarda attractive and then she became so infatuated with the masked gentleman who turned out to be that dreadful Lord Merton and now here she was dreaming of a dalliance with Mr. Chandos.

Perhaps it was because she was so far away from the life of study at Fenfold and perhaps this was just what happens to a young lady with nothing better to occupy her mind – she falls victim to storybook love!

Yet she was helpless in its grip and she had no one to turn to for guidance.

She was so alone – alone with this growing passion for the elusive Mr. Chandos.

As if he sensed her train of thought, he turned from his perusal of the sea.

In a shaft of moonlight his eyes gleamed at her.

Was there just a hint of that expression that had so intrigued her?

She would never be sure, for at that very moment an unwelcome voice rang out in the stillness of the night.

"Mr. Chandos!"

Both Mr. Chandos and Leonora turned to see Mrs. Griddle approach, a ship's lantern in her fist.

"I've been looking for you all over, Mr. Chandos," she puffed, throwing a suspicious glance at Leonora.

"For me?" questioned Mr. Chandos calmly.

"Yes." Mrs. Griddle put her free hand on her breast as if to still its motion. "I'd remarked on your displeasure at my giving Desiree a slap on the wrist. I felt I should explain my action lest I appear too cruel a mother."

She glanced again at Leonora before continuing,

"It's just that I don't wish Desiree to *brood* on the subject of love. You see, in London she was involved with a penniless young man, quite undesirable in the opinion of her father and me. We had someone far more suitable in mind, but our Desiree refused to even countenance him and continued to slip out to meet her young man.

"In the end we decided the only course open to us was to remove her entirely, and that is what we have done. The sea is a mighty divider, as I'm sure you'd agree, Mr. Chandos! And Desiree's heart will soon mend, particularly if we find her a more suitable match!"

She held the lantern high and peered meaningfully at Mr. Chandos who rewarded her with the same silence he had maintained throughout.

Leonora, however, who had listened in mounting rage to Mrs. Griddle's self-righteous soliloquy, could not contain herself.

"Surely you wouldn't force your daughter to marry a man she does not love against her will!" she exclaimed.

Mrs. Griddle's mouth dropped open at this outburst and the hand holding the lantern shook a little.

Mr. Chandos regarded Leonora coolly.

"You sound just as if you are speaking from bitter experience, Miss Cressy," he said softly.

Leonora reddened.

"I am."

Their mutual gaze locked for a moment before Mrs. Griddle recovered her voice.

"I knew it, young lady. You've run away from an arranged marriage. Oh, how could you? You must surely understand that in these matters *your parents know best.*"

Leonora swung round, stung.

"On this occasion my stepfather most decidedly did *not* know best!" she retorted hotly. "All he was interested in was the fact that my proposed husband was rich. He didn't care a jot that my suitor was as – as unattractive and unprincipled as himself!"

"My goodness!" exclaimed Mrs. Griddle, glancing at Mr. Chandos. "What do you mean by 'unprincipled'?"

"Just as I say," replied Leonora defiantly. "He was a man who had lived so long in some foreign country that he might simply *buy* himself a wife in England!"

"I presume you had some conversation with him," remarked Mr. Chandos, still staring at the waves, "to have discovered him to be so without redeeming features?"

"I danced with him once, but we barely conversed. It was only later that I realised his true nature."

"*His true nature?*" repeated Mr. Chandos.

"*Yes.* He – he frequented Clubs of ill-repute – and bartered for me over a game of cards."

"Dearie me!" exclaimed Mrs. Griddle.

"Yet it might have been better to actually meet him after he bid for your hand," persisted Mr. Chandos, "before pronouncing so on his ill qualities."

"I did not need to meet him – " persisted Leonora defensively, wondering why he should be so partisan on behalf of someone he had never met.

"The mere fact that my stepfather championed Lord Merton's suit was quite enough."

She could have bit her tongue as she realised that she had revealed the name of her erstwhile suitor.

Mrs. Griddle's eyes widened.

"You turned down the proposal of a *Lord?*"

"She did," came Finny's voice.

No one had noticed his approach. He stood now at Leonora's elbow, shawl over his arm.

"She said she'd rather marry Lord Merton's horse, as it ain't so *old* and *grizzled*!"

"Oh, Finny," Leonora murmured reprovingly.

It then struck her that Mr. Chandos might actually be acquainted with Lord Merton.

Mr. Chandos detached himself from the rail.

"You must please excuse me, ladies, from further participation in this enlightening conversation as I do have some work to complete in my cabin."

He gave a bow and strode off along the deck.

Her heart miserable, Leonora watched him go.

Mrs. Griddle also stared after him.

"What work can he need to do, I would wonder? He brought nothing on board with him."

"He didn't need to," Finny then offered cheerfully, oblivious of his previous indiscretion. "He has everything in his cabin already. Books, writing desk, ink and paper. He has clothes too – shirts, cravats and leather boots."

"Indeed?" Mrs. Griddle looked thoughtful. "And I thought he had decided to travel at the last moment. I am glad to say that I stand corrected. A man of purpose is by far the more preferable suitor."

Leonora heard her with a sinking heart.

There was no doubt that Mrs. Griddle had plans for Mr. Chandos and meanwhile she had no doubt blotted her copybook forever in his eyes!

"Finny, I think I shall retire."

"I'll see you to your cabin," suggested Finny.

Mrs. Griddle's eyes narrowed as Finny then offered Leonora his arm.

She considered it quite improper for a cabin boy to take such liberties with a passenger and was astonished that Leonora did not reprimand the fellow.

'I must mention all this to Mr. Griddle,' she said to herself. 'It may be that we should discourage intercourse between Miss Cressy and Desiree! Miss Cressy seems far too ready to disregard Social distinctions.'

Leonora might have been amused if she had been privy to Mrs. Griddle's thoughts.

As it was she received Finny's arm gratefully as she suddenly felt a little unwell and was glad of the support.

Finny led her proudly away. Though he played the role of cabin boy well, he considered his true position on board to be that of guardian to Miss Leonora.

Leonora did not then look back at Mrs. Griddle, but leaned heavily against Finny.

She knew that it was no use scolding him for his indiscretion in front of Mr. Chandos.

Her mother had once told Finny that he must learn to 'bite his tongue' in company. He had taken the caution literally and made his tongue bleed! He had not thought like others since he fell out of a tree as a boy and landed on his head!

The ship gave a sudden lurch and Leonora clutched Finny more tightly.

"I don't feel – quite myself," she confessed.

"I'll go bring you hot water and sugar."

In her cabin, Leonora sank gratefully onto her bed. Finny knelt to remove her shoes and then tiptoed from the cabin as she lay back against her pillows.

"Thank you so much, Finny," she mumbled as the cabin door closed behind him.

She thought of Mr. Chandos, working away in his

cabin across the narrow corridor and she was glad that he could not see her now. Her forehead was hot and she was sure her face was flushed.

She heard footsteps outside – it could not be Finny returning already with the hot drink he had promised.

The footsteps stopped outside her door.

The doorknob was turning, slowly and quietly. She raised herself on an elbow, staring anxiously.

"W-who is there?" she called.

"A devoted admirer!" came the unexpected reply.

The door then opened and there to her astonishment stood Señor de Guarda, a tumbler of whiskey in his hand.

Leonora stared at him in dismay.

"What do you want?" she asked in a low tone.

Señor de Guarda shrugged.

"Company. It is lonely on deck. I hate the sea and the sea knows it, for what does it do, but send a great wave crashing over me."

Leonora closed her eyes for a moment as the ship gave a sudden plunge.

"Well, I am afraid I am not fit company for anyone at the moment," she muttered truthfully.

Señor de Guarda swirled the whiskey tumbler.

"I know. I pass that boy on his way to fetch you a drink." He eyed her curiously. "When I meet you at the dock, this – Finny is your servant. Now he is a cabin boy. How is this?"

Leonora felt her elbow grow weak.

"Someone found him the situation," she answered. "It was none of my doing. Someone who obviously took an interest in him."

"Or in you," murmured Señor de Guarda.

Leonora felt very ill now. Her elbow gave way and she slid down in the bed.

Señor de Guarda regarded her for a second and then came towards her.

Sitting on the bed, he put his free hand on her brow. She shrank away from his touch, turning her head sideways on the pillow.

Her door was still open and as she looked, the door of the cabin opposite opened and Mr. Chandos stepped out.

As if in a dream she saw his gaze settling on the scene before him – Señor de Guarda bending over her as she lay prostrate.

Mr. Chandos's eyes rested coldly on Leonora's face for an instant and then he was gone.

Leonora gave a moan of despair.

"There, there," mumbled the Señor.

She struggled up.

"Go away. You should not – have come in here."

He threw up a hand and rose.

"Forgive me, lovely lady. I was just thinking you needed some comfort. Another time, eh?"

Winking, he then blundered out of the cabin.

Leonora fell back, tears coursing down her cheeks.

Mr. Chandos could not but misinterpret all he had seen. She was utterly compromised in his eyes now! He must think her an utter fool. To set herself up as a girl who rejected the suit of a Lord only to encourage the advances of a trader in whalebone!

Not that it would matter what Señor de Guarda was if she *loved* him, she told herself.

Hearing Finny approaching, she hurriedly dried her eyes on the edge of the sheet.

"Here you are now, miss. Hot water and sugar with a dash of lemon. That'll settle you for the night."

He held Leonora's head while she drank.

"Better, now?" he asked.

"A little," she lied.

She did not feel better at all. Her stomach churned, her limbs ached and her heart felt heavy as lead, so she lay back and Finny drew the cover over her.

"Don't go yet," Leonora pleaded. "Talk to me."

"I can't stay long, miss. I've got to turn down the beds in the other cabins."

"Will you be preparing Mr. Chandos's bed next?"

Finny nodded.

"His sheets are all silk, miss. And he has a velvet counterpane. *And* embroidery on his slippers."

Leonora pricked up her ears.

"Embroidery? What does it look like?"

"It looks like those things on carriage doors – "

Leonora drew in her breath.

An insignia! So Mr. Chandos *was* connected to the aristocracy. In which case he must know of Lord Merton's family if not personally acquainted with him.

How could she have been so silly as to divulge the details of her story to all and sundry?

"Do you like Mr. Chandos?" she asked Finny.

Finny looked strangely furtive.

"I likes his boots, and he gave me sixpence when I brought him tea."

"But – would you consider him a man of honour?"

Finny turned the question over in his head.

"He's important," he said at last. "Otherwise how could he have done what he did for me?"

Leonora gave a start.

"What *has* he done for you, Finny?"

Finny's eyes grew large with sudden alarm.

"Why, I didn't mean – he made me swear – it just slipped out – I didn't mean to say it at all."

Witnessing his confusion, she understood at once.

"It was – Mr. Chandos you met at the docks, wasn't it? It was he who found you this work on board!"

Finny, eyes darting to all corners, rose to his feet.

"I have to go, Miss Leonora – my duties."

"Finny!" called out Leonora sharply. "Sit down."

"I mustn't – I mustn't – "

Without a backward glance, Finny flew to the door, opened it and was gone.

Leonora placed her hand over her eyes.

So it was indeed Mr. Chandos who had taken pity on Finny when the trap had almost lost a wheel.

Mr. Chandos who had heard Finny's tale and found a solution to his unwillingness to return to Schilling House.

So it was Mr. Chandos who was responsible for the fact that she had the company of Finny on this voyage!

In which case, she realised, Mr. Chandos probably knew her story right from the start, for Finny would have told him the reasons why she was leaving England.

One thing she was sure about was that he would not have mentioned that she had taken Mr. Schilling's money.

She knew Finny well enough to know he would not disclose information that might make his Mistress appear in an unfavourable light.

Why Mr. Chandos wished his act of charity to be kept a secret, she could not imagine, unless he wished the extent of his influence on board the ship to go unnoticed.

Perhaps, she thought with a sudden thrill, he has his own sad story to relate.

Perhaps he too is fleeing an unhappy experience of love. He had after all talked about her reminding him of 'someone very dear'.

Her next thought plunged her into dismay.

If Mr. Chandos had fled an unhappy love affair, he had soon recovered. How else could he have then devoted so much attention on Desiree Griddle?

He has a shallow heart indeed, she brooded bitterly.

Yet he was so handsome, so enigmatic with such dark and intelligent eyes, such a strong physique.

She began to toss and turn on her bed.

She wished she could banish Mr. Chandos from her mind, just so that she could sleep.

Next the floor suddenly arose, as if a creature was attempting to force its way in from below.

Leonora gripped the edge of her bed as she seemed to feel her stomach turn upside down within her.

"Ohhh!" she groaned.

She found herself wishing, despite the memory of her revolting stepfather, that she was now back at Schilling House, back in her own room with its window overlooking the garden – safe and *still* in her own dear bed.

She felt so alone.

If only she had not frightened Finny away with her questions. If only – oh, if only her dear Mama was here.

Or Isobel, her friend Isobel, whose cool hand would sooth her brow to cajole her out of this obsession with Mr. Chandos – how she would gently chide her for losing her head in this irresponsible way.

She had heard that love was a sickness and so it was. Why the very blood in her body seemed to be on fire.

This cabin was too stuffy.

She could bear it no longer. She needed air, air to blow her fevered thoughts away like so much thistledown.

Struggling to sit upright, she swung her feet over the edge of the bed and felt for her shoes and shawl.

She groaned, heaved herself to her feet and opened her cabin door.

Her progress along the corridor and up the stairs was unsteady.

As the ship ploughed unruly waves, Leonora clung to walls and banisters. She never knew how she made it to the deck, but next she pushed through a heavy door and there she was.

She had imagined a fierce wind blowing, but the night was strangely still and it was only the sea that reared angrily beyond the rail.

Leonora staggered to a bench and dropped down, clutching her shawl about her.

The brisk salty air was welcome and after a while she felt a little revived.

She was leaning her head, staring out into the night, when a slight movement caught her eye. She turned and what she saw made her heart sink as deep as the sea.

Mr. Chandos and Desiree stood in the shadows of the over-hanging upper deck, his arm was clasped around her, whilst her head – that head with its pall of dingy hair – was leaning most intimately on his shoulder.

Sick to her soul, Leonora rose and stumbled away, back to the dark confines of her cabin and a web of stormy bitter thoughts.

CHAPTER SEVEN

Leonora had no desire the next morning to go to the dining salon for breakfast, instead she asked Finny to bring coffee and bread rolls to her cabin.

She had not slept well, plagued as she was by the recurring image of Desiree Griddle in Mr. Chandos's arms.

She had bunched up her pillow, sighed loudly and wept quietly as the night crawled by.

Finny looked concerned when he saw that she had barely touched the bread rolls.

"You'll look just like a broomstick when you arrive in Brazil," he grumbled as he took up the tray.

"Don't scold me, Finny, I have no appetite."

She waved her hand in a gesture of weary dismissal and Finny turned to go.

"They was asking for you at breakfast," he said.

Leonora's heart gave a faint leap.

"W-who, precisely?"

"Señor de Guarda and that Mr. and Mrs. Griddle."

"Oh," whispered Leonora.

"Is there anything else you need, miss?"

"Was no one else at the table?" she persisted.

"No. But the daughter came in later – the thin girl with the lanky hair."

"Was she – alone?"

"Yes, miss. She had red eyes and a red nose!"

Leonora, despite herself, gave a sudden giggle.

"Oh, Finny. You always cheer me up, do you think she has a cold?"

"She might have, miss. She had a big handkerchief with her. It was one of Mr. Chandos's. I recognised it 'cos it had that emblem on it."

Leonora turned her head away quickly.

"I wonder how she came to have it?"

"She and Mr. Chandos were a-talkin' on deck quite late last night. Maybe he gave her the handkerchief then."

"Does the whole world know about that late night tryst?" she asked with a hint of peevishness.

Finny looked at her in surprise.

"I don't think so. I only know 'cos Mr. Chandos told me."

"*He told you?*" echoed Leonora in disbelief.

"Yes, miss. I was laying out his night things when he came in. He started untying his cravat and then he said 'Finny, I've just spent a troubled hour on deck with Miss Griddle. I don't mind telling you that I take a great interest in that young lady's future'."

Leonora sank back on her pillows.

So he had spent a *whole hour* with Desiree – and a *troubled* hour too, and then he was ready to openly declare his interest in her!

It was too much to bear!

She had determined to spend the morning in bed, trying to catch up on sleep, but realised after a few minutes that she felt too restless.

She also realised that she no longer felt ill. Perhaps the coffee had settled her stomach and at least the ship was not lurching about in quite such a violent fashion, so she decided that she would pass the time writing to her mother.

She felt somewhat ashamed as she took up her pen as she had almost forgotten about her poor dear Mama in the emotional turmoil of yesterday and today.

'*Yesterday and today,*' she repeated with a shock.

It had taken less than two days for her to be totally discomposed by Mr. Chandos! It just seemed beyond the bounds of possibility that she should be in the grip of such passions in so little time.

'*I am not now who I was*', she decided. 'It must be because of all that had happened in the last few weeks.

'What a great deal I have experienced already,' she thought with a sudden proud thrill.

'What a great deal I have experienced and survived. Why, I shall survive this passion for Mr. Chandos too, and Isobel and I will laugh at my folly over scones and cream, or whatever it is they have for tea in Brazil!'

She began to write to Mama, describing everyone on board, even going so far as to tell her a little about Mr. Chandos, but not revealing the true extent of her interest.

Leonora had by now filled up four pages and might have continued on, but she heard the gong sound for lunch.

With a wild flourish she signed herself "*your loving Leonora*", sealed the letter and put it aside to be posted.

She still did not wish to go to the dining salon and rang for Finny. He was delighted that she felt hungry and hurried off to fetch her soup and fruit from the kitchen.

She finished everything on the tray and after lunch decided she needed some fresh air.

She put on her cloak and went up to the promenade deck, taking a book with her and was relieved to see that there was no one about.

After a stroll she sat down and opened up her book and soon found that she could not concentrate.

The glitter of the sea drew her eye, the screech of gulls drew her ear and the book lay abandoned on her lap.

A familiar figure stepped between her and the sun.

"Ah! Miss Cressy! You are feeling better?"

Leonora sighed inwardly.

"Thank you, yes, Señor de Guarda.

"I am so glad to hear it." He gestured at the empty chair to the right of Leonora. "May I – ?"

Leonora blinked as, without waiting, he sat down.

"You missed an excellent lunch, Miss Cressy," he remarked, leaning rather intimately towards her. "Fish pie. Sherry trifle. What an institution is sherry trifle!"

Unwilling to be drawn into conversation especially one on the subject of sherry trifle – Leonora said nothing, but took up her book again.

Señor de Guarda was not to be discouraged.

"Ah, you are trying to read. What is this called?"

Reaching over her, he took hold of the book.

Leonora froze in horror at this act of audacity.

"Miss Cressy," then came the rasping voice of Mrs. Griddle. "How good of the Señor to lure you away from your cabin. You have been rather hiding yourself!"

Leonora turned her head in a daze to see both Mr. and Mrs. Griddle, staring down at herself and the Señor.

Beyond them Desiree lingered with Mr. Chandos, whose eyes burned as they settled on Leonora.

She flushed as she realised that Mr. Chandos had yet again seen her in a somewhat compromising proximity to Señor de Guarda.

98

When she next looked up, Mr. Chandos had already averted his gaze, so she stared with longing at his profile, forgetting her determination to expel him from her heart.

She started as Mrs. Griddle tapped her shoulder.

"Well? Where have you been all morning?"

"I – have been rather unwell – "

"Then no doubt Señor de Guarda's attentions have reinvigorated you," added Mrs. Griddle sarcastically.

Leonora was unnerved.

She looked pleadingly towards him for a rebuttal of Mrs. Griddle's comments, but he seemed merely amused by her discomfort.

"Miss Cressy is reinvigorated not by me, but by her reading. Her book is very very serious."

"Oh?" Mrs. Griddle looked down her nose at the book in Leonora's lap. "And what is the subject matter?"

"It's about life – in a mining town," she replied.

She was aware of Mr. Chandos turning to stare at her and felt her blush deepen.

Mr. Griddle frowned down at the book.

"Not at all a suitable subject for a young girl!" he pronounced. "I'd never allow Desiree to read such books."

"There's nothing left at all that I *can* read," moaned Desiree, "since you won't allow me romance either."

"There's the Bible," sniffed Mrs. Griddle, "and the hymn book. They should be sufficient for any young girl."

Desiree said nothing more and Leonora almost felt sorry for her until Mr. Chandos spoke up on her behalf.

"I am sure Miss Griddle would benefit from a wider literary repertoire. I have some volumes of poetry with me that I am sure she would enjoy."

"Well," deliberated Mrs. Griddle, "if *you* then, Mr.

Chandos, consider it respectable for a young girl to read such matter as poetry – "

"I do, and I should be glad to lend her my books."

"Perhaps you would guide her in choosing which of the poems to study?" suggested Mrs. Griddle slyly.

"With pleasure," he replied, glancing at Desiree.

Leonora was most aggrieved to witness the looks that passed between the two. It was most *conspiratorial*, she decided and now Desiree would have a good reason to seek out the company of Mr. Chandos.

Mrs. Griddle looked vaguely around the deck.

"I think we should all sit down and order some tea."

Except for Mr. Chandos everybody took a seat.

Leonora was unsettled to have Desiree sink into the vacant chair on her left.

"You and I have had so little opportunity to become acquainted," the girl whispered.

Leonora shifted uneasily in her chair – she had no desire whatsoever to become acquainted with the object of Mr. Chandos's attention.

Mr. Chandos was standing with his back to the rail and she supposed bitterly it was just so that he might gaze unhindered at Desiree in her silly straw bonnet!

"Are you keeping a lookout for the Steward, Mr. Chandos, so we can order tea?" called Mrs. Griddle gaily.

"I am indeed," he replied, but he turned his head neither to left or right, continuing to stare towards Desiree and, by default, Leonora.

Desiree sighed deeply into Leonora's ear.

"Mr. Chandos is such a singular gentleman!"

"Is he?" she responded dryly. "I had not noticed!"

"Oh, but surely you have!" insisted Desiree. "He

has such noble bearing. Like a Prince or something. And yet he is so very kind."

"I had never considered that a Prince might *not* be kind," observed Leonora haughtily.

"No, I suppose not, but that Mr. Chandos should so interest himself in – *me*, I consider a great compliment."

"And I am sure it pleases your mother *greatly*."

Desiree blushed and fell silent.

Leonora was cross with herself. Desiree had given the impression of wanting to confide in her. Had she only held her tongue she might have learned something about the situation between her and Mr. Chandos.

Though what good would *that* do her.

She regarded Desiree from under lowered lids.

What could possibly excite the interest of any man in her she could not fathom? Desiree really was as pale as ash. She seemed to have no eyelashes at all and her lips were thin, as if someone had sketched in the mere idea of a mouth with a red pencil. And her expression –

Leonora was just about to tell herself that Desiree's expression was becoming insipid to say the least when a sudden change came over her features.

Her eyes began to widen, her lips began to tremble, and a slow pink flush rose into her cheeks.

Had Mr. Chandos made an amorous signal to her?

Leonora turned her head to see –

Mr. Chandos still stood with his back to the rail, but he was no longer alone. With him stood a young man who was quite evidently a member of the ship's crew. He was not a Steward, for his face was smeared with coal dust, his shirt was torn and there was soot in his tangled beard.

"What is that fellow doing on the passenger deck?" exclaimed Mrs. Griddle. "He's a stoker!"

"Curious," Señor de Guarda agreed.

Leonora was puzzled as the young stoker seemed transfixed at the sight of Desiree! There was no doubt that his intense stare had made her agitated.

What *was* it about little Miss Griddle that had such an effect on men?

"What is he gawking at?" continued Mrs. Griddle angrily. "Mr. Chandos – tell him to take himself off. He should not be here."

"I feel I should point out, Mrs. Griddle, that this is not a passenger deck. The crew are at quite at liberty to pass this way if they so choose."

Mrs. Griddle, disconcerted, fell back in her seat.

"Did I not say, Mr. Griddle," she grumbled, "what we should be exposed to if we embarked on a cargo vessel! To be stared at by such riff-raff – a filthy looking fellow!"

From Desiree came a repressed sob and Leonora regarded her in astonishment.

The young stoker looked uncomfortable.

"I meant no harm at all," he mumbled. "I was on my way below deck when I saw – I saw – "

"You saw *me*," interposed Mr. Chandos. "You have a message, do you not?"

"That's right, sir. A message from – from – "

"From the Captain?"

The stoker nodded eagerly.

"Yes, sir. From the Captain."

He pressed a crumpled paper into Mr. Chandos's hand and then with one glance at Desiree, he stumbled off.

Mr. Chandos did not read the message, but tucked it into his pocket, staring after the stoker all the while.

Leonora noticed that Desiree as well stared after the

stoker, her handkerchief to her lips as if she was afraid of letting out some inadvertent exclamation.

'What role does the stoker play in the affairs of Mr. Chandos and Desiree?' now wondered Leonora. 'Is he the means of passing secret messages between them?'

"Eccentric of the Captain to send such a chap with the message and not a Steward," Mrs. Griddle was musing. "I declare – this vessel is run in a most peculiar way."

"You should complain to the Captain himself, then, dearest," soothed Mr. Griddle. "For here he comes."

"How opportune!" cried Mrs. Griddle.

Mr. Chandos moved quickly to greet the Captain. The two men talked for a few minutes in low voices and then they came on towards the group of seated figures.

"Captain, I have a bone to pick with you – !" began Mrs. Griddle.

"Ah, yes," smiled the Captain, with a quick glance at Mr. Chandos. "You object to my choice of messenger, I believe. Well, madam, I do apologise, but on a cargo ship one does not always have the right man to hand.

"Of course, Mrs. Griddle," the Captain went on, "I understand how upsetting it all is to a lady so careful of the usual proprieties as your good self."

Mrs. Griddle simpered as Mr. Chandos turned away and Leonora was certain she had detected a grimace cross his features.

"I hope you will not object, Mrs. Griddle, when you learn that I myself have come in the guise of messenger," the Captain continued.

"Oh, I couldn't, I wouldn't!" fluttered Mrs. Griddle. "After all, you do not sport a filthy beard and you are not covered in soot!"

Desiree put her face in her hands and her shoulders gave a little shake.

Leonora hesitated and then her better self prevailed, as she laid a gentle hand on Desiree's arm.

Desiree looked up, her eyes brimming with tears.

"So what message is it you bring, Captain?" Mrs. Griddle asked sweetly.

"Well, I have decided to throw a party this evening. It will be only a modest affair, but there will be punch and entertainment provided by the professor and his family."

"All the passengers are invited?"

"Of course and though there are not many of you, I hope it will prove a convivial affair."

"I am certain that all present here will accept with alacrity," pronounced Mr. Griddle.

Leonora was disconcerted that she had accepted on her behalf. She was not at all sure she wanted to attend a party when Mr. Chandos and Desiree were sure to further cement their attachment.

There was also the question of what to wear. How could she appear at the party in yet another of her mother's old-fashioned and ill-fitting gowns?

She then bit her lip, wondering if she might make her excuses on the grounds of poor health, but the Captain was already moving away.

Desiree was looking at her anxiously and seemed to read her thoughts.

"You will come along this evening, won't you?" she pleaded. "I should so welcome the company of another young lady."

Leonora regarded Desiree coolly.

"But Mr. Chandos would not welcome the presence of a companion, surely?"

"Whatever do you mean, Miss Cressy? Surely you don't think – "

Before Desiree could complete her sentence, Mrs. Griddle's voice rang out loudly.

"Here's the Steward at last and thank Heavens too. We're all nearly parched to death. Now, what shall it be? Darjeeling and muffins?"

Amid the flurry of orders Señor de Guarda took the opportunity of addressing Leonora.

"I hope you will dance with me this evening, Miss Cressy?"

"I don't think I will dance with anyone."

"I will endeavour to change your mind – "

Tea arrived and as everyone settled down with their cups and plates, Mrs. Griddle returned to the subject of the Captain's invitation.

"He might call this evening 'a modest affair', but I for one will seize the opportunity to dress my family and myself in style. I have brought along a particularly pretty wardrobe for my daughter. I always make sure that she is always dressed *à la mode*. Would you not agree that I am successful in this, Mr. Chandos?"

Mr. Chandos looked up. His eyes flickered towards Desiree, who sat in mute embarrassment at being singled out for attention.

"I am sure that Miss Griddle pleases many an eye."

"But one eye more than the others?"

Mr. Chandos hesitated.

"One eye more than others, indeed, madam."

Mrs. Griddle swooned.

"Yet you must agree that I might be permitted to guess, Mr. Chandos?"

"Indeed you may," he replied dryly.

Leonora listened to this chatter with her head bent

105

over her cup. It seemed odd that Mr. Chandos was willing to declare his interest in Desiree to Finny, but not to her mother. Perhaps he was not entirely serious in his suit?

Would he be so cruel, though, as to lead Desiree to believe he had intentions when he did not?

"Well," added Mrs. Griddle. "I always endeavour to make Desiree the belle of the ball."

"You certainly do," beamed Mr. Griddle, turning casually to Leonora. "And what will you be wearing this evening, my dear?"

"I am not – sure. All my dresses need – alteration. In fact, I was wondering if Mrs. Griddle would be able to lend me a sewing case."

She then gestured wearily to Leonora.

"Come to my cabin later, Miss Cressy, and I shall endeavour to provide you with what you need."

At this juncture Leonora decided to slip away to her cabin. There she spread all her dresses out on the bed and spent much time deciding which one she should single out for the evening.

At last she chose a midnight blue silk. There was little she could do about its high forbidding bodice, but she could shorten the hem and cut off the unflattering bow.

*

At six o'clock she went in search of Mrs. Griddle's cabin and found it crammed with trunks, some of which lay open to reveal mountains of hosiery.

Desiree lay still on her bed, a cold compress on her forehead, her hand thrown up behind her on the pillow.

She had obviously been crying, for her eyelids were swollen and inflamed.

As Leonora hesitated in the doorway, Mrs. Griddle gestured at her daughter.

106

"I don't hold with all these afflictions of the heart, Miss Cressy. It's unhealthy. No, don't come in, you might tread on some tissue. I'm just trying to repack our goods."

As Mrs. Griddle twittered on, Leonora glanced over in wonderment at Desiree. What sort of 'afflictions of the heart' could reduce the girl to this?

Surely her budding relationship with Mr. Chandos was not responsible?

Mrs. Griddle thrust a green pouch at Leonora.

"There you are. Reels of cotton and some needles. A pair of scissors. That should do you."

"Thank you," said Leonora as she was pushed out of the door. "Goodbye, Desiree."

She heard Desiree murmur something from the bed as the door closed behind her.

In the sudden dark of the corridor, she found herself suddenly uncertain of which way to turn.

She blundered along until she saw a light ahead, so she hastened her steps and rounded the corner.

The light shone upwards from a lower deck.

She peered over the rail and then withdrew a little, as if afraid to be seen.

There below her was Mr. Chandos in what seemed like a heated conversation with the same stoker who had so agitated Desiree.

As Leonora watched the stoker suddenly turned and punched the wall, drawing his fist away to reveal bloodied knuckles.

"Don't be a fool!" she heard Mr. Chandos shout.

Trembling she turned around and stumbled blindly back along the corridor.

She was quite clear as to what she had witnessed.

The two men were quarrelling over Desiree. The stoker had punched the wall rather than Mr. Chandos, who had remained cool as he was certain of his ground.

Desiree was *his* – if he so desired.

Leonora reached her cabin and flung open the door. She moved in a daze to the centre and just stood there.

She felt herself rise and fall gently with the ship and after a moment she realised that she was clutching something to her breast.

What was it?

She held it at arm's length for a good minute before she remembered.

Mrs. Griddle's sewing pouch.

So then tonight Desiree would be the belle of the ball, loved by two men while she was loved by none!

CHAPTER EIGHT

Leonora surveyed herself dubiously in the mirror.

Despite her bad mood, she had worked quickly to alter her mother's dress. The hem was now just right and the large bow had been removed, but she had not had time to attack the collar that made her look like a Governess!

Then there was her face.

She could pinch her cheeks until they flushed pink and she could brush her hair until it shone, but how could she put a sparkle into her eyes?

She sighed and turned away from her reflection.

What did it matter how she looked?

Who was going to notice her, except Mrs. Griddle, and *her* eye would be merely critical?

She opened the cabin door and came face to face with Señor de Guarda, his hand raised as if about to knock.

"Miss Cressy, you look, how is it to be said? Most singular. I am hoping you will allow me to escort you?"

He crooked his arm and waited.

Leonora stared at him – the Señor, of course!

He might not actually *love* her, but there was no doubt that he *admired* her, even in her present strange garb.

He had certainly striven to look his very best with his glistening moustache and impeccably pressed trousers.

Better to enter the salon in his company than alone.

"I shall be most happy Señor," she murmured, and took his arm.

Bunting had been hung around the salon and a long trestle groaned with various dishes.

In one corner of the room the professor and his sons were setting up music stands and taking two violins from their cases, while his wife was dusting down the piano.

Mr. Griddle was already sampling the buffet, whilst Mrs. Griddle stood at his side, waving a garishly painted fan rather violently before her face.

She was encased in a stiff magenta coloured gown and Leonora thought she looked like a mushroom!

The Captain advanced with a smile.

"Miss Cressy, Señor de Guarda. I am very happy you could join us. I hope you will partake of our excellent buffet and the splendid punch in the tureen over there."

"I shall fetch two glasses immediately," said Señor de Guarda enthusiastically.

Leonora was barely aware of the two men moving away together, for her mind was elsewhere as she sought out Desiree and Mr. Chandos.

Mr. Chandos was not to be seen, but there Desiree was, sitting on a wooden settle.

Dressed awkwardly in an unbecoming lime green, she was playing with the clasp of her gold purse. Now and then she cast a furtive look at her mother.

Leonora frowned.

What was in that purse that she fidgeted so with it?

Desiree seemed unaware of Leonora as between the purse and her mother her attention was utterly consumed.

Until, that is, there were murmurs in the doorway of the salon.

Desiree turned her head to the sound and suddenly her whole face brightened.

Leonora with her back to the door began to tremble, as she had no doubts as to the identity of the new arrival.

She hardly dared look and yet she could not resist.

Yes, it was *he*!

Oh, how divine he looked in his dark coat and silk cravat. He was by far and away the most handsome man in the room – on the ship – in the world!

What was more, he was looking at her. Directly at her! And there was something in his gaze that she had not expected.

Beneath heavy brooding eyelids his expression was tender and appreciative.

Leonora's pulse quickened as he made as if to step towards her.

Then almost immediately something stopped him in his tracks. His features hardened and he turned abruptly away as at the same moment a voice sounded in her ear.

"Your drink, Miss Cressy."

It was Señor de Guarda.

In a daze she turned round to receive the glass he proffered. Out of the corner of her eye she could see Mrs. Griddle snap shut her fan and heard her declare that there was a place for Mr. Chandos on the settle beside Desiree.

Numbly she sipped from the glass and spluttered,

"What is this? It's rather strong for my tastes."

"Why, it's punch, Miss Cressy."

"There's – rather a lot of it."

"You will soon grow to like it, take another sip."

"It's not unpleasant," she admitted.

"Indeed not," he replied. "It is full of goodness –
there is plenty of fruit in it, you see – to prevent scurvy."

"Scurvy?"

"You must take plenty of it, at least four glasses for
a lady."

Señor de Guarda watched her with amusement as
she drained her glass and held it out for more.

"I am glad to see you develop a taste for it, since it
will do you so much good."

As he then made his way over to the buffet table,
Leonora could not resist turning once again in the direction
of Desiree and Mr. Chandos.

To their obvious discomfit, Mrs. Griddle was now
hovering above them like a hawk.

The professor and two his sons, encouraged by the
Captain, began to play.

Both Desiree and Mr. Chandos looked hopeful as
Mr. Griddle advanced on his wife to ask her to dance. But
Mrs. Griddle shook her head and threw meaningful glances
at her daughter and Mr. Chandos.

It was as though she was not going to relinquish her
guard until he had actually declared his intentions.

The matter was taken out of her hands, however, by
one of the ship's Officers, who presented himself with a
bow to Desiree.

Mrs. Griddle gave out a squawk as Desiree, after a
slight nod from Mr. Chandos, rose up to accept the young
Officer's invitation to dance.

Leonora held her breath as they took to the floor.

Why had Mr. Chandos countenanced this move?

Her question was answered at once, as he stood up
and made his way over to her.

"I should be very delighted, Miss Cressy," he said solemnly, "if you would dance with me."

Leonora's lips parted, but no sound came.

Was it possible that he had dispensed with Desiree in order to be free for her, Leonora?

"Miss Cressy?"

Leonora swallowed and glanced towards the buffet table to see Señor de Guarda turning back with two full glasses of punch in his hands.

This decided her.

She must accept quickly or Señor de Guarda would surely intervene.

Lowering her gaze, she held out a trembling hand.

Mr. Chandos took it and a shudder ran through her, as his hand was so warm, his clasp so firm.

She felt so weak at his touch she wondered how she would be able to dance.

Then Mr. Chandos, in one move, crushed her to his breast. His strength flowed into her and suddenly there seemed only air beneath her feet.

It was ecstasy to be in his arms!

There were but three musicians, yet it seemed as if a whole orchestra was playing.

Her heart swelled with joy.

The neglect she had felt at his hands was forgotten.

His espousal of Desiree was forgotten.

For this moment he was hers and hers alone.

His arm now encircled her waist, his fingers were entwined in her fingers.

She began to lose all sense of time and place.

It was almost as if she was back at Broughton Hall

all those weeks ago in the arms of the masked stranger, so similar was the sensation.

She did not dare raise her face as she was sure her features would reveal her emotions.

And she could have sworn that Mr. Chandos was not unmoved himself as his hold tightened by the minute.

His lips brushed her temples and she felt his breath on her hair.

"Look at me," he whispered.

Leonora lowered her head still further.

"No, look at me."

Lips trembling, she slowly lifted her head.

His eyes could have scorched her skin, so intense was his scrutiny!

They almost stopped dancing and just stood there, swaying, locked in this mutual and burning gaze.

"Miss Cressy!"

The voice that intruded was all too familiar.

Mr. Chandos loosened his hold as Leonora turned a dazed face to Mrs. Griddle's tart expression.

"I am sure, Miss Cressy, that Mr. Chandos has no desire to keep you from the company of your *actual* escort for this evening, Señor de Guarda here."

The Señor regarded Leonora wryly.

"Here is me, Miss Cressy," he said, pulling a long face. "Abandoned – after all our little intimacies."

Mr. Chandos visibly whitened as he stepped back, his hands tightening at his side.

Leonora repressed a cry of despair.

The spell was broken and broken so cruelly. How could she explain that Señor de Guarda had no claims on her at all, had never received any encouragement from her, and had no hold on her whatsoever?

She threw a beseeching glance at Mr. Chandos, but he would not look at her.

"Excuse me, Señor de Guarda, I return Miss Cressy to your protection," he mouthed stiffly.

Mrs. Griddle gave a victorious smirk as he bowed and moved away.

"I expect an announcement at any time," she said to Leonora. "Look he is going straight to my daughter now."

Leonora followed her gaze numbly.

Yes, Mr. Chandos was bowing to Desiree and yes, he was drawing her onto the floor, his lips at her ear just as they had been at hers but a while before.

Mrs. Griddle turned to cast a last triumphant glance at Leonora and it was in that second that Desiree quickly took a folded note out of her purse and slipped it into Mr. Chandos's hand.

Leonora could not believe her eyes.

What kind of man *was* Mr. Chandos, to enflame her emotions as he undoubtedly had during their dance and a moment later accept what was most certainly a *billet-doux* from another young lady?

It was that *billet-doux* in her gold purse that had so obviously agitated Desiree all evening!

She felt a glass thrust into her hand.

"Drink up, Miss Cressy," urged Señor de Guarda.

"Yes, drink up," echoed Mrs. Griddle as she moved away. "I'm sure it is an habitual occupation for you."

Leonora gasped aloud.

She was so distracted by this casual insult that she forgot the part Señor de Guarda had played in destroying her character in front of Mr. Chandos.

"Don't mind," the Señor was saying now as he put his hand under Leonora's and guided the drink to her lips.

"You will see, this will lift your spirits. For you are a little cast down, I think."

Leonora gave a strangled laugh.

"Yes, I am a little cast down!"

"Well, then. Drink."

'I will drink,' thought Leonora. 'I will drink till my heart feels warm and carefree and then I won't care for Mr. Chandos or anyone else.'

In this spirit she downed the glass and then sent Señor de Guarda for another.

She wanted Mr. Chandos to see that she was quite capable of enjoying herself whether she was the focus of his attention or not.

But Mr. Chandos was now nowhere to be seen and in trepidation, Leonora looked for Desiree.

Had she disappeared too?

No, Desiree was sitting where she had sat for most of the evening – on the settle, purse clasped in her lap.

The third glass of punch did not bring the desired effect and Leonora's heart felt no more warm or carefree than before, whilst the Señor plied her with yet another.

When her head started swimming, he gripped her elbow and steered her quickly towards the door, advocating a dose of fresh air.

Leonora found herself propelled to the upper deck.

She stood blinking in the bright moonlight while he made sure that the door that led below was fast closed.

Leonora craned her neck and gazed up at the sky. Stars hung like dim pearls in the inky darkness.

She forgot all about Señor de Guarda.

From the salon strains of music wafted to her ears and she imagined she was still in the arms of Mr. Chandos.

Slowly she began to turn as if she was dancing, her arms held out at either side for balance. As she turned, her eyes passed over the shadows below the giant funnel and she could have sworn there was a figure there, watching.

A figure that stepped immediately back.

She did not stop to wonder who it was, but turned again, head thrown back, her slender white neck exposed.

Señor de Guarda lurched towards her and then sank to his knees.

"My blood, but you're beautiful!"

Leonora, halted in her solitary dance, stared down as he grasped her hand and brought it to his lips.

"How I have waited – " he groaned.

Disliking the feel of his kiss on her skin, Leonora tried to draw her hand away, but his grip tightened.

She winced, feeling that he was crushing her bones.

"Don't!"

In answer he dropped her hand and flung his arms around her skirts instead.

Leonora pressed a hand to her forehead.

"Don't!" she pleaded again.

Señor de Guarda gave a snarl.

"It is time, señorina, to bestow your favours on *me*! Remember I know enough to undo you."

With horror Leonora felt his hand grasp her ankle and begin to slide up along her calf.

A figure stepped from the shadows with a roar.

"You are a cowardly dog, sir!"

She had no time to wonder at hearing the voice of Mr. Chandos, as the Señor thrust her from him cursing.

She stumbled back – reached for the rail – missed it and fell.

Striking her head on the deck, she knew no more.

*

She felt as if she was swimming upwards through murky water. All around her was dark, but there above her a faint light flickered and she struggled towards it.

Then a dark shape seemed to come between her and the light and she felt a hand on her forehead and wondered how that was possible.

Was there someone else with her in these depths?

Now she felt something damp placed on her brow.

"Leonora?" she heard a voice murmur.

She blinked back into focus and turning, she stared straight into the anxious eyes of Desiree Griddle.

"Thank Heavens! You have been unconscious for some time."

'*Unconscious*!' thought Leonora. She gave a groan as the memory of what had occurred on the deck flooded through her.

Now everyone would know what a fool she was!

Raising a hand, she felt her forehead. Yes, there on the right was a large bump, tender to the touch. Her whole head still throbbed somewhat.

She wondered if Desiree had witnessed Señor de Guarda's improprieties.

Had there been *two* figures in the shadows?

She scanned Desiree's face for a hint of scorn, but found nothing to show that she thought any the less of her than before.

She must, however, make sure.

"W-what happened?" she asked tentatively.

"Mr. Chandos found you lying on deck. You must have fainted and hit your head as you fell."

Leonora turned quickly away to hide her relief as another thought struck her,

"H-how did I get back here, to my cabin?"

Desiree leaned forward to straighten the wet flannel on Leonora's brow.

"Mr. Chandos carried you down."

Carried her! Leonora's head swam. She had been in his arms, clutched to his breast and had not known it!

If only she had regained consciousness enough to feel, if just for a moment, the beat of his heart close to hers.

Yet if he had carried her down, he had not stayed to tend her. He had rather left her to the ministrations of her rival, a fact she suddenly resented.

"How did you come to be here?" she now queried Desiree narrowly.

"Mr. Chandos sent Finny to fetch me. He didn't want Mama or any of the other passengers to know what had happened, particularly as Mama is liable to become hysterical at the slightest opportunity.

"Mr. Chandos knew that I would be the best person to attend you," Desiree added with an air of such innocence that Leonora was quite thrown.

She seemed so blissfully unaware of the animosity that she, Leonora, harboured towards her.

Perhaps she is a little stupid, thought Leonora, with bitter satisfaction.

This thought was the only bit of comfort she could draw from the whole experience, for she was only too well aware of how low her reputation must now stand in the opinion of the man she had so wished to impress.

She shuddered and closed her eyes as she recalled that humiliating scene on deck.

From the shadows, Mr. Chandos had witnessed her dancing in front of Señor de Guarda. She had behaved in a wanton fashion and no doubt Mr. Chandos considered that this had provoked the Señor's assault upon her.

Tears welled underneath her lids. She tried to force them back but failed as they trickled down her pale cheeks in such profusion that Desiree was alarmed.

She ran swiftly to the cabin door and opened it.

"Finny!" she called out along the corridor.

Finny had obviously been nearby, for he was there in an instant.

"Yes?" he enquired. "Is Miss Leonora all right?"

At the sound of his voice, she opened her eyes.

"Yes – I'm all right Finny."

Desiree looked dubious.

"Perhaps you might bring something warm for her to drink, Finny?" she suggested.

"A little soup if I can get cook to heat it up?"

"Yes, that would be good, but Finny, don't be long, will you? Because it's – getting late, isn't it?"

"Nearly midnight, miss, but I won't be long."

Finny hurried away.

"Midnight – midnight," Desiree muttered to herself.

She sat down, put an abstracted hand on Leonora's brow and immediately sprang up again.

Small as the cabin was, she began to pace the floor and seemed for a moment to have forgotten her charge.

Leonora watched, a bitter suspicion in her breast.

It was obvious that Desiree had an assignation that she was most anxious to keep.

An assignation with Mr. Chandos! That had been the meaning of that *billet-doux* in her purse that she had finally managed to slip to him.

'I won't let her go,' Leonora suddenly resolved. 'I know it is hateful and petty of me and it won't make Mr. Chandos love me rather than her, but – *I won't let her go!*'

Her mind made up, she began to moan loudly.

Desiree stopped her pacing and stared at Leonora.

"What is the matter?" she cried. "Are you in pain? Shall I fetch the Captain? He is, I think, a doctor of sorts."

Leonora shook her head and held out her hand.

Desiree came close and grasped it.

"My poor friend!" she murmured.

If some flush of shame ran through Leonora at this designation of 'friend', she quickly suppressed it.

All is fair in love and war.

She could not *win* this war, for it was obvious that Mr. Chandos had already made his choice, but she could take a perverse pleasure in making sure the path of love did not run too smoothly!

She closed her fingers around Desiree's hand.

"I am sure I'll be all right if you don't leave me," she pleaded, allowing tears to well in her eyes again. "I d-don't want to be alone. Please don't leave me."

Desiree looked fraught.

"Not leave you?"

"No – if you are truly my friend – "

"Oh, I am, I am," insisted Desiree, though her eyes flew hither and thither as if to find a means of escape.

"Then stay with me."

Desiree hesitated for a short moment and then in resignation, let her head droop.

"Of course I will, at least, until you sleep."

'*Until I sleep,*' Leonora echoed silently, 'very well, I *won't* sleep!'

She was helped in this resolution by the return of Finny with a bowl of hot soup, but she sent him away lest Desiree should find his presence an excuse to leave her.

She enlisted her aid in sitting up and asked her to hold the bowl while she drank from the spoon.

She noticed with satisfaction Desiree's expression grow more and more miserable by the second.

She finished the soup and lay back on the pillow.

The light rocking of the ship was soporific and she soon found herself having to fight to keep awake.

"Tell me about yourself, Desiree," she urged.

"Oh, there is nothing about me that would interest someone like *you*, Leonora. I'm really quite ordinary, you know. And – plain."

'Surely not too ordinary or plain for Mr. Chandos,' Leonora thought bitterly.

"I'm really not that talented, either," she continued. "Though I am good at needlework."

"You are too modest," said Leonora wryly. "After all, you've had your share of admirers, haven't you?"

Desiree looked sad.

"Not many, no."

"Not one who was – is – special?"

"Y-yes," she faltered. "One who *is* – special."

'*Ha,*' thought Leonora, '*she's as good as admitted it*! It is Mr. Chandos, for the only other admirer is the one her parents prised her from by carrying her off on this ship and *he* could only be referred to in the past tense!'

Desiree now seemed to have relinquished all hope

of attending her assignation. Hands folded on her lap, she stared silently down at the floor.

Regarding her wretched expression, Leonora began to feel uncomfortable. After all, it was little more than a trivial triumph to boast that she had prevented the lovers meeting on just this one occasion.

'How far I have come from the girl at Fenfold,' she pondered with concern. '*She* would never have stooped to torment someone like Desiree in this way.

'*She* would never have so demeaned herself as to drink punch and dance in front of a man whose character is as questionable as that of Señor de Guarda.

She shivered as she recalled his threat.

"*Remember I know enough to undo you!*"

He knew that she was a runaway and he knew she had taken Mr. Schilling's money – in fact he knew enough to ruin her reputation on this ship and beyond.

Leonora sighed to herself.

'What would Mama say if she knew? What would Isobel say?'

Isobel would certainly reprimand her. 'How could you let *love* change you so for the worse?' she would ask.

Leonora was brought out of her punishing thoughts by the sound of a knock at the cabin door and she watched as Desiree went to the door and opened it.

Mr. Chandos stood outside.

Glancing to the right and left along the corridor, he handed Desiree a folded piece of paper.

She took it and scanned it quickly before thrusting it into her bodice and then looked up at Mr. Chandos and said something in a low voice.

In an equally low voice, he replied. Desiree shook her head and twisted her hands in apparent anguish.

She turned to refer to Leonora where she lay in bed and Leonora quickly closed her eyes.

When she opened them a few seconds later, Desiree was writing something at the table.

She then returned to the door, where Mr. Chandos waited, and handed the paper to him.

They are making yet another assignation, Leonora thought angrily, her moment of remorse quickly forgotten. They have no shame!

"You may depend on me," she heard Mr. Chandos say quietly and then he was gone.

Desiree closed the door and returned to her chair.

"Are you awake?" she asked Leonora.

Leonora, as if asleep, turned to the wall.

'I'll wait and see what she does next,' she promised herself, stifling a yawn. 'I won't sleep, I'll just wait.'

The very late hour proved too powerful for her for a second, however, but the next thing she knew was that her eyes were wide open.

Raising her head, she saw that the cabin was empty.

Desiree had gone.

Crossly she sat up and felt for her shoes. She must have slept for just an instant and in that instant her quarry had flown.

She then stumbled to the door, opened it and looked along the corridor, just in time to see the edge of Desiree's skirt disappear around the corner.

Driven to distraction at the thought of them meeting after all – though hardly knowing what she would do if she should indeed so discover them – Leonora hurried after.

To her surprise, Desiree did not seem to be making for the saloon or deck or anywhere that Leonora deemed appropriate for a secret meeting.

Instead she was heading for the stairs that led down to the lower depths of the ship – normally out of bounds to passengers.

Leonora waited until she heard Desiree's steps ring out on the steel stairs. Then she ran to the rail and peered after her.

She would have to take off her shoes if her pursuit was not to be discovered as she followed Desiree.

The very air below seemed to pulsate and Leonora realised she must be near to the engine room.

What on earth could have possessed Mr. Chandos to suggest such a rendezvous?

For a second her resolve faltered. What could she possibly hope to achieve by following Desiree in this way?

The misery of seeing all her suspicions confirmed? The mortification of seeing that pallid creature wrapped in the arms of the man that she, Leonora, desired more than any other in the world?

Did she hope such a sight would act as a purgative on her emotions and rid her of this ridiculous obsession?

Hearing Desiree reach the bottom of the stairs, she gave herself a shake.

There was no time to dwell on her motives.

She was cast now upon her course, as surely as a leaf on the surface of a stream.

Taking firm hold of the steel rail of the stairway to steady herself, she started down.

CHAPTER NINE

The heat became stifling and the thrum and throb of the engine was like the beat of a gigantic heart.

The cladding of the ship seemed to shudder and she tried not to think of the dark mass of sea on every side.

She found herself in what seemed for the moment like the centre of a volcano. It was all fire and noise, fierce glow and cavernous shadows.

Her face burned with the heat emanating from four huge furnaces.

The furnaces in turn were like the gaping maws of hungry beasts. Stokers in dirty vests, sleeves rolled to the elbow, slaved to feed them with shovelfuls of coal.

Leonora cast frantically round for Desiree.

The pounding furnaces created avenues as straight as the boulevards of a foreign City and along one of these Desiree was creeping, her head low as if trying to hide.

Near the end of the row of furnaces she stopped and drew from her bodice the *billet-doux* that Mr. Chandos had given her earlier that night.

Leonora watched jealously as she brought the paper to her lips before reading its contents again.

Once read she thrust the paper back into her bodice, and proceeded on turning left at the end of the row.

Although her footfall could not possibly be heard amidst the din, Leonora found herself resorting to tiptoe as she followed quickly after her prey.

There was a series of doors in a long wall and one of these was open and there stood a stoker, his hair lank over his forehead, his hands holding a tin mug.

He seemed unaware of Desiree, who had stopped in her tracks at the sight of him.

Leonora, her view impeded somewhat by the figure of Desiree, shrank back to observe the scene before her.

She felt a degree of satisfaction at the idea that this humble stoker with his tin mug might prove an unwitting obstacle to the fulfilment of the lovers' plans.

Obviously Mr. Chandos waited behind one of those very doors that Desiree did not dare now approach!

Then the stoker heaved an audible sigh and shifted his weight from one foot to the other.

Trembling, Desiree now moved closer to the wall, leaning against it for support. This gave Leonora a clearer view of the stoker and what she saw made her start.

She recognised the same soot-streaked features of the young man she had once suspected of passing messages between Mr. Chandos and Desiree. The same young man she had later seen punch the wall during a heated exchange with Mr. Chandos.

Whatever the nature of his role previously, Leonora decided scornfully, he was now playing the part of look-out to warn the lovers if someone might approach.

Again she contemplated turning back while she was still unobserved.

Another second and all her certainties were shaken.

Desiree, her eyes still fixed on the stoker, suddenly gave out a low moan, whether of frustration or sorrow, she could not determine.

It was a sound the stoker could not possibly have heard amidst the noise and yet he looked Desiree's way.

Seeing her, he gave a cry, threw the mug aside and rushed forward.

Leonora gasped as she saw him sweep Desiree into his arms and press his grimy face to her pale cheek.

What was this? Where was Mr. Chandos?

Was Desiree playing false already?

Playing false with a mere crew member, a fellow in a torn vest with a dirty face? How *could* she?

The dirty stoker was now swinging Desiree around in undisguised ecstasy.

In this circuit Desiree's eyes fell on Leonora and opened wide in alarm. She then struggled to release herself from the stoker's grasp.

Alerted, he set her down and Desiree pointed.

There was pause before the stoker found his voice.

"What the hell do you mean by this?" he demanded of Leonora.

She was astounded at his lack of embarrassment, as she had indeed witnessed a most compromising encounter.

"What do *I* mean?" she replied haughtily. "Isn't the question rather, what do *you* mean, sir?"

The stoker's response was not at all what she might have expected.

"That, young lady, is my business."

Leonora smarted with indignation.

His business? As if Mr. Chandos did not exist, as if he had no prior claim on this young woman who now so heartlessly and heedlessly betrayed him!

"I would think Mr. Chandos might not agree with you there," she retorted acidly.

Desiree and he threw each other a glance.

"Mr. Chandos?"

Leonora felt a little disconcerted to see that the two looked puzzled and not guilty at the mention of Desiree's erstwhile suitor. Nevertheless, she blundered on,

"Yes. Does *he* know about this assignation?"

Desiree regarded her gravely.

"Of course he knows about it, Leonora. It's *he* who has been helping us."

"*Helping* you?"

"Yes. Robert and I could not meet openly so then Mr. Chandos carried messages for us."

Leonora could not believe her ears, at both hearing Desiree refer to the stoker by his first name, and at the idea of Mr. Chandos playing Cupid.

Robert was regarding Leonora with a frown.

"Was it some misplaced concern for Mr. Chandos that made you follow Desiree here?"

Leonora swallowed. Now that she was being forced to account for herself, she found that there was no way she could throw a favourable light on her behaviour.

"Desiree was – kindly looking after me – and I was worried when she disappeared," she murmured, feeling that this explanation had the virtue of not being entirely untrue.

"I did disappear, but thought that you were asleep," began Desiree, when Robert put his finger to his lips and beckoned the two girls to follow him.

Leonora could hear the sound of someone testing the pistons of a nearby machine.

She hesitated, unwilling to be implicated further in this strange web of deception, but Desiree quickly grasped her hand and drew her along.

Robert closed the door quietly behind them.

"Perhaps a little tea to calm our nerves?" he asked.

Leonora barely heard as she looked dazedly about her. She took in a tin kettle on a stove, a large trunk and four bunk beds covered with brown blankets.

Robert followed her gaze.

"I share this room with three other fellows."

Desiree gave an appalled cry.

"Oh, Robert, it's so small!"

"I don't mind. I am now used to it. I'd put up with anything for you – you know that, Desiree."

Leonora flinched instinctively as matters must have now gone far between them.

"I really don't feel I should remain here," she said, glancing at the door.

"Oh, please stay," pleaded Desiree. "Robert only wanted us to come in here in case someone saw us."

"That's right," confirmed Robert. "My room-mates are all right. They are in on the secret, but should the Chief Engineer get wind of what's going on – "

He trailed off and looked away, suddenly uncertain. Leonora waited a moment and then turned to Desiree.

"So what exactly *is* going on?" she asked, unable to disguise a hint of disapproval.

Desiree reddened as she caught Leonora's tone.

"It's not – what you may think, Leonora! This isn't something unconsidered or flippant. The truth is – Robert and I – we're engaged. We've been engaged for some time, only Mama wouldn't countenance it and took me away."

Leonora paled as she remembered Mrs. Griddle's revelation that she was going to Brazil in order to remove Desiree from an unsuitable suitor.

Robert with his tangled beard was that 'suitor'!

And she had thought that Desiree was in love with Mr. Chandos!

'What an utter fool I have been! *An utter fool*!'

"Miss Leonora?" Robert was now looking at her in alarm. "Perhaps you should take a seat?"

Leonora sank gratefully down on a nearby stool.

Her thoughts were in turmoil as she watched Robert pour water into a teapot while Desiree looked for mugs and she could not but notice Robert's longing glances at her.

'*I considered her so insignificant*,' she reproached herself, '*but look how he loves her*!'

There was silence as he filled the mugs with tea.

"So how did you manage to be on the same ship as Desiree?" Leonora asked Robert at last.

He thrust his fingers into his beard.

"Mr. Chandos – " he replied, glancing at Desiree.

"Mr. Chandos?" repeated Leonora feeling that there was no end to the surprises in store for her.

Robert gave a nod.

"I'll tell you the whole story from the beginning. When I learned that Desiree's parents were planning to take her abroad and away from me, I determined to follow. I'm not at all a very brave fellow, but I wasn't going to let my one chance of happiness be stolen from me.

"So I contrived to discover the name of the ship she would be travelling on and the date it was sailing with the intention of finding employment on board.

"I disguised myself by growing this beard, although it was not really necessary. Mrs. Griddle had only agreed to meet me the once to tell me that I was unsuitable – I was only a clerk in a publishing house, you see.

"I came down to Bristol in order to visit the Offices

of the Steamship Company, saying I wanted to sign on for work. They laughed at me at first, saying I did not look strong enough, but then Mr. Chandos came in and wanted to know what was going on.

"I then decided to tell him my whole predicament and once he'd heard me out he hired me on the spot."

"*He* hired you?" Leonora's eyes widened. "What authority had he to do that?"

Robert gave a disbelieving chortle while Desiree's eyes turned with astonishment on Leonora.

"Bless you, Leonora," he cried. "Don't you know, Mr. Chandos is the owner of this ship?"

Leonora swayed on her stool.

"H-he is?"

"Sole owner. He had a partner once, but the partner died. He owns a mine in Brazil and that's where the steel girders in the hold are going. He's a very wealthy man."

Leonora was now beyond absorbing any more. Her mind was running in a fever back over the last few days.

She had indeed noticed the deference shown to Mr. Chandos by the Captain and the crew, but there had been no other sign of his importance.

He had never pulled rank and it was obvious that none of the other passengers realised his status.

Now she could understand that meeting on deck in the moonlight, when Desiree had rested her head on Mr. Chandos's shoulder and now she appreciated his chivalrous interest in Desiree.

He was the confidant and go-between.

When he had offered to lend her books, it was no doubt to facilitate the exchange of messages with Robert and when he had taken the note from Desiree in her cabin, it had been destined for Robert, not for himself.

"You can depend on me," he had said and Leonora had interpreted those words as a lover's pledge.

'Oh, fool, fool,' she cried desperately to herself. 'I have snubbed and ignored him out of jealousy when all the time he was acting at the urge of his generous heart.'

She could not prevent herself from groaning.

"Are you not well, Leonora?" asked Desiree.

"I am – fine, I am just tired. It must be very late."

Robert threw a glance at Desiree.

"It is," he admitted glumly.

Leonora understood the situation at once. He was hoping for a little time alone with Desiree.

"Excuse me, I really must be going now."

"Should I not accompany you?" ventured Desiree.

"Not at all. I will find my way back. I feel fine and I'm sure you two have – much to say to each other."

As Robert opened the door and looked warily out, Desiree caught at Leonora's arm.

"You won't tell Mama?" she urged in a whisper.

"Oh, Desiree, do you really think I would?"

Desiree, relieved, shook her head.

"And I won't tell on you – "

She blinked as she realised Desiree was promising not to inform Mr. Chandos that Leonora had felt obliged to intervene tonight on his unwitting behalf.

"Thank you," Leonora murmured.

Desiree smiled wanly as Robert, having ascertained that the coast was clear, ushered Leonora out.

*

Mr. Chandos was not at breakfast the next morning and neither was Desiree.

Mrs. Griddle threw Leonora a questioning look as she sat down, but was otherwise reasonably forthcoming. She said that Desiree was feeling unwell.

Finny was serving at breakfast this morning and he fussed over Leonora, much to Mrs. Griddle's interest.

Leonora was not hungry, but under Finny's watchful eye, she forced herself to eat a boiled egg.

When he went off to serve another table, however, she threw down her napkin and quickly excused herself.

She did not want to return to her cabin just yet and went instead to the upper deck.

Who should be there, leaning on the rail and staring at the horizon, but Mr. Chandos!

Now that she knew his true character and the depth of his kindness to Desiree and Robert, she felt even shyer of him than ever.

Her heart fluttered as she approached him.

"Good morning, Mr. Chandos."

"Good morning, Miss Cressy."

She hovered, twisting the end of her shawl.

"You were – not at breakfast?"

"No. I was not hungry."

Leonora bit her lip and turned to stare at the sea.

"It is – very fine today," she murmured at last.

Mr. Chandos nodded.

"Fine now, yes, but I really don't like the look of that dark horizon."

There was indeed a black line of cloud lying low where the sea and sky met.

"Does it mean a storm?"

"I hope not."

Silence fell again between them.

Leonora did not know how to broach the subject of last night's unhappy incident with Señor de Guarda and yet broach it she must, if only to thank Mr. Chandos for his timely intervention.

At last she cleared her throat.

"M-Mr. Chandos?"

To her considerable dismay she felt she detected an impatient sigh as he turned to face her.

"What is it, Miss Cressy?"

His eyes were dark and their expression unfriendly.

"I-I wanted to thank you, Mr. Chandos, for carrying me to – my cabin last night."

He waved her words away with a frown.

"Any gentleman would have done the same. There is no need to thank me."

"Oh, but there is!" she carried on bravely. "I know that you interceded when Señor de Guarda – "

She faltered as she saw the effect the Señor's name had on Mr. Chandos. His eyes grew hard and a muscle in his jaw flexed.

"You had better say no more, Miss Cressy, I should not wish you to compromise yourself still further."

Leonora started.

Compromise herself?

She knew that she had behaved foolishly with the Señor, but surely Mr. Chandos did not believe that she had encouraged his attentions to the degree of assaulting her?

"I know that you overheard all that passed between Señor de Guarda and me, Mr. Chandos. In which case you must be aware that I did not – welcome his attentions?"

Mr. Chandos's expression was glacial.

"It did not *seem* you welcomed it, no, but who is to say what sort of conduct finds latent favour with a lady?"

"L-latent favour?"

"In retrospect, in the safety of your cabin, Señor de Guarda's appeal grew and what had frightened you at the time began to intrigue you – enough for you to rise from your sickbed to seek him out, no doubt to further test what his Latin arts of seduction might bring about."

"I – don't know what you mean."

Mr. Chandos gave her such a look of contempt that she felt she must wither before him.

"I brought the Captain to your cabin to see if you were recovered, Miss Cressy. He has medical knowledge, but unfortunately we found your bed empty."

Leonora gasped in dismay.

Mr. Chandos had obviously expected Desiree to be absent from the cabin, but not herself, the patient he had carried unconscious in his arms.

He knew that Desiree had an urgent assignation, but he could only guess where she, Leonora, might be and with whom and that he believed she had returned to the bosom of the Señor was a blow to her self esteem.

All she had to do now was tell him the truth and he would be mortified at his mistake.

But how could she reveal her secret?

How could she tell him that she had suspected his interest in Desiree to be amorous?

How could she possibly explain to him that she had followed Desiree out of jealousy?

She lifted her hand weakly.

"I assure you, you are – mistaken," she whispered.

"Am I, Miss Cressy?" His tone cut her like a knife.

"Well, perhaps Señor de Guarda will throw some light on the matter, for here he comes."

Leonora turned to see the Señor bearing down on them with an expression of penitence on his face.

His features underwent a transformation, however, as he detected the charged air about her and Mr. Chandos. He became at once alert, his eyes moving swiftly from one to the other.

"Miss Cressy, Mr. Chandos," he said with a bow.

Mr. Chandos looked at him with disdain.

"I am surprised, sir, that you feel so free to appear in public after your conduct last night!"

Señor de Guarda's eyebrows rose.

"You English – you take courtship so seriously."

Mr. Chandos snorted.

"Courtship, you call it!"

"I was just a little rough in my approach, perhaps, but the ladies like it, you know. If you had not considered it right to interrupt, who knows but that Miss Cressy might have been persuaded to humour me a little – "

"As no doubt she did later!"

Leonora's hands flew to her face, whilst Señor de Guarda narrowed his eyes with interest.

Whether or not he knew just what Mr. Chandos's words meant, he was quick to jump on what they implied.

"Ah," he sighed. "Whenever has a young woman been consistent in her attitude? Whomever she loathes one minute, she embraces with a full heart the next."

He winked at Leonora.

"Isn't that so, my little bird?"

Mr. Chandos swung away with a muffled curse as Leonora gave a strangled cry.

"I am not – *your little bird*!"

Señor de Guarda's eyes flashed such a warning that Leonora shrank back.

"Oh, but you are, my dear," he insisted. "You are my little *magpie*, are you not?"

Leonora understood in an instant.

Magpie. The *thieving* magpie. He was reminding her that he knew of her past. He was reminding her that he knew she had taken Mr. Schilling's money.

It was clear that if she refuted his version of their relationship, he would not hesitate to expose her there and then to Mr. Chandos.

Her eyes filled up with tears of rage that even now, after such a long interval of time, the odious Mr. Schilling should still be casting such a shadow over her life.

A shadow that now lay wide as the Gulf of Arabia between her and Mr. Chandos. There was no crossing it.

His friendship was lost to her, *lost*!

She must feign a bond with Señor de Guarda or let her reputation be ruined.

The Señor held out his arm.

"Come, Miss Cressy. We have so many things to talk about this morning."

Eyelids lowered and trembling, she took Señor de Guarda's arm and he led her triumphantly away.

She felt Mr. Chandos's cold gaze on her back.

"You keep forgetting that I know you for what you are, Miss Cressy," the Señor muttered as soon as they were out of earshot. "Just look here!"

Leonora turned her head numbly to see him fumble in his waistcoat and then draw out a leather pouch –

Mr. Schilling's pouch!

"W-where did you get – that?"

"I just don't know where *you* were last night, Miss Cressy, but I know where *I* was. In your cabin, whence I had come to offer my apologies! Finding you gone, I took the opportunity of securing this – memento of your past."

"You are a thief!"

"Precisely, my dear magpie. It is *exactly* why I feel we are destined for one another."

Leonora stopped and pulled her arm from his.

"Destined for one another? Señor de Guarda, once we arrive in Rio, I want *nothing* more to do with you."

He showed his teeth.

"Rio is indeed a small place compared to London, Miss Cressy. I can ruin your reputation even more easily there. You are in my power and that is how I want it.

"I find you most desirable. I am going to have you and I don't want you to encourage Chandos's attentions. You must promise me this or else – !"

Leonora stared at the ground.

"I don't need to promise. Mr. Chandos has not the slightest interest in me."

He gave a grunt.

"If you believe that, all to the good. Now excuse me. I must deprive you of my company. I am due to play cards with Mr. Griddle."

Leonora raised her eyes to watch him go, her mind and body seething with dislike.

Whilst she remained on board, she would have to abide by his strictures. How she would get away from him once in Rio she did not know, but get away she must.

She moved as if in a trance to her cabin.

She imagined Señor de Guarda now feeling free to fawn over her in public, kissing her hand, taking her arm, carrying her hat – all under the eye of Mr. Chandos, who already had such a low opinion of her!

She could not bear it! She *would* not bear it! She would refuse to appear in public at all.

She would feign illness and remain in her cabin for the rest of the voyage.

And she would ask Desiree to play nurse, so if the Señor came calling, she would not be alone!

She pushed open the door of her cabin and, closing it behind her, allowed her emotions free vent.

Tears flowed down her cheeks as she heard again those harsh words of Mr. Chandos!

"As no doubt she did later – "

How could she rest until she had absolved herself in his eyes? She *must* tell him where she had been last night.

Far better that he suspect her of jealousy towards Desiree than unseemly conduct with the Señor.

She crossed to the small writing table and sat down.

"Dear Sir," she wrote,

"I wish to tell you the truth about where I was last night and why.

Faithfully yours, Leonora Cressy."

She folded the letter and rang for Finny.

When after five or so minutes he had not appeared, she went to the door and opened it.

The corridor outside was quiet and she hesitated for a second and then stepped out.

Moving quickly she stooped to slide the letter under Mr. Chandos's cabin door.

As she did so, the ship gave a sudden lurch and she put her hand on the door handle to steady herself and the cabin door swung slowly open.

Straightening herself she stared in at his room.

He had obviously not returned from his sojourn on deck for the room was empty.

Leonora took a step forward.

Another step and she was across the threshold. As if mesmerised, she circled the cabin, touching every item that was so intimately connected with him.

His dressing gown, thrown across the back of a gilt chair. His hairbrush and ebony comb. His half-open trunk. His silk cravats, his gloves. His writing case.

His writing paper with its embossed letter head.

The letter head!

Leonora stared down, arrested, the breath knocked from her body as if by a mortal blow.

She recognised the crest.

She had seen it before – on the side of a carriage as it drew away from a light-filled house.

And even if she had not recognised it, there below was a name that she did.

Arthur Chandos, the Lord Merton.

The gentleman she had danced with at Broughton Hall, and the man she had danced with here on board ship, were one and the same!

The man from whose embrace she had fled was the very man whose good opinion she now vigorously sought.

He had known who she was all along and he had deceived her!

With a cry of despair, she crumpled the letter in her hand and fled.

CHAPTER TEN

Each swell of the sea seemed higher than the last.

Leonora sat on her bed, her forehead on her knees, her thoughts racing.

Everything began with the tiny chiahuahua –

If she had not scooped up the dog that day outside the *Black Jack Inn*, then Lord Merton, no doubt newly arrived in England, would never have noticed her.

If he had never noticed her, he would never have pursued her and she would never have fled her home.

She lifted her head and brushed away a tear.

Lord Merton – Arthur Chandos – one and the same!

A gentleman who was so determined to get his own way, he had tried to *purchase* her from her stepfather.

'But why *me*? Why should Lord Merton have been so keen to pursue *me*?'

There was no answer to that question.

He clearly operated on the kind of acquisitive whim that infected many of his class, who always believed they could buy whatever they wanted.

It was indeed a kind thought of his to bring a gift from Brazil for a relative – whoever that might be.

It was kind of him to find a job for Finny and kind to help Desiree and Robert, but she suspected an ulterior motive in all these scenarios.

She was groping in her reticule for a handkerchief

when the cabin lurched at an acute angle and her stomach turned over.

She remembered the thin line of dark cloud that Mr. Chandos – Lord Merton – had pointed out on the horizon.

'I wonder if the storm has hit us,' she worried.

Finny put his head round the door.

"That sea's got mighty rough, miss. Mrs. Griddle and some of the other passengers are now in the salon. I'd thought you might be scared and should join them."

Leonora hesitated. She had resolved to remain out of the reach of Señor de Guarda, but the thought of being tossed about alone in her cabin was alarming.

Retrieving her shawl, she rose and stumbled after Finny. The floor heaved beneath her and she had to steady herself with a hand on each wall of the corridor.

Finny caught and helped her through the swinging doors when they reached the salon.

There they all sat, some looking rather greener than others. Tables had been laid for lunch, but it was clear that nobody would be eating.

Leonora noticed Desiree lying with her eyes closed and her head in her mother's lap.

Mr. Chandos – Lord Merton – oh, what *was* she to call him now? – stood apart, his eyes fixed on the turbulent waves assaulting the windows.

He seemed lost in anxious thoughts.

To Leonora's relief, there was no sign of Señor de Guarda as Finny settled her onto a chair near Mrs. Griddle.

Leonora glanced at Mr. Chandos and then away.

'*How I hate him now*!' she decided.

Yet the next moment her eyes strayed to him again.

A Steward came in with a telegram, looked round, and moved unsteadily towards the figure at the window.

Mr. Chandos turned at his approach and took the telegram.

Despite herself, Leonora watched him curiously as he opened the telegram.

His grim expression relaxed a little as he read the contents and then, as if sensing Leonora's rapt appraisal, he raised his head.

Too late – she blushed as his eyes met hers.

His dark eyes flared for a second and then he came towards her, the telegram open in his hand.

"Miss Cressy," he began. "I really must apologise for approaching you after our last unhappy meeting, but I have something here – "

He stopped abruptly as Leonora leaped to her feet.

"I don't wish you to address me – *ever*!" she cried.

Heads turned as she pushed past him and ran from the salon. Outside she turned first one way, then another, before finally dashing up some stairs.

She had no idea where she was going, only that she was running from a man who deeply disturbed her.

Her heart pounded wildly as she pushed against a heavy door at the top of the stairs and fell into the storm.

Her skirt billowed out round her and salt spray was as sharp on her face as particles as ice.

She did not want to turn back for fear that he had followed her.

'If I can keep hold of the rail,' she thought, 'I shall surely make it to that door at the other end of the deck.'

She started, but the rail was freezing to the touch. The wind whipped along the deck and seemed determined to force her back. Soon she was making no headway at all.

A hand reached out and caught her arm.

She could not see who it was, but she instinctively struggled to free herself.

To no avail.

She was drawn roughly back into some shelter and there someone shook her hard by the shoulders.

"You silly little fool! Don't you realise you could be washed overboard in this weather?"

Recognising Mr. Chandos's voice, she then shook wet strands of hair from her face and stared angrily at him.

"I shall go wherever I please," she retorted. "And when I please. You are not my Master."

His eyes flashed.

"By Heavens, if I were your Master, I'd beat some manners into you!" he blazed.

Leonora had no time to answer as the ship pitched so suddenly that she was thrown hard against his breast, so hard that she gasped.

She felt the stuff of his waistcoat against her cheek and felt his breath on her hair as he stooped to support her.

The next moment her blood began to pulse wildly, as wildly as the sea that beat against the prow of the ship, for Mr. Chandos had thrown his arms around her and was murmuring into her hair – words that were almost but not quite carried away by the wind.

"I *will* win your favour, I *will* make you love me. It is not in my nature to yield once I am set on a course!"

She fought an overwhelming desire to succumb.

"You delude yourself!" she cried loudly. "I might once have imagined myself in love with Mr. Chandos, but I could never, never love Lord Merton of Merton Abbey, for that is who you are, isn't it? And Lord Merton *I hate*!"

Shocked, he released her and once again she turned on her heels and fled.

This time she was not pursued. She made it to her cabin, flew through the door, locked it and flung herself on her bed.

'I just want to sleep!' she moaned. 'I don't want to think about Mr. Chandos or Lord Merton – or that odious Señor de Guarda – or Mr. Schilling. I just want to *sleep*.'

As if in response the ship abruptly ceased its frantic plunging and fell into a gentle rock like a baby's cradle.

Whether or not it heralded the lull before a greater storm, Leonora did not consider.

She closed her eyes and the world faded away –

*

When she awakened some time later, it was to the sound of frenzied bells and the corridor outside her cabin echoed with pounding footsteps.

Someone hammered on the door.

"To the lifeboats! To the lifeboats!" was the cry.

Leonora then sat up with a jolt. Her lamp was out and the cabin was in darkness.

She felt for the floor and grimaced as her feet sank an inch deep into water.

Stumbling towards the door, she opened it and then drew back in horror.

Seawater was now swirling along the corridor and even as she looked, the momentum intensified.

Her blood chilled as someone far away screamed.

Mr. Chandos's door was open, but he was not there.

She began to wade towards the stairway. Her skirt was soon soaked and its weight impeded her. Water was cascading down the stairs. Gripping the handrail, she tried to pull herself up, but the strong water forced her back.

Far above her on deck, she heard whistles blowing.

The passengers and crew had taken to the lifeboats and forgotten her.

She was going to die!

Driven by sheer terror, she renewed her attempts to mount the stairs.

Halfway up, she slithered and fell.

She was still struggling to regain her foothold when someone caught her under the arms and lifted her.

She was carried upwards through a torrent of water.

"W-what has – happened?" she asked weakly.

"The ship was approaching the Azores when it was carried onto rocks," came the reply close to her ear.

Leonora recognised the voice of Mr. Chandos even as he set her on her feet in front of one of the lifeboats.

His gaze swept across her and she blushed as she realised that she was in her petticoat, which clung damply on her, accentuating the delicate curves of her figure.

Her bodice had slipped down, revealing a creamy white shoulder and she fumbled instinctively to draw it up.

She was forestalled, as Mr. Chandos put out a hand and gently pulled the bodice in place.

Then he was gone, striding off to help three sailors lower one of the two starboard lifeboats.

Before there was time to marvel that it was he who had rescued her yet again, her attention was distracted by the sound of loud shrieking.

Sailors scrambled around on the listing deck, busy securing ropes to the other starboard lifeboat, in which the professor and his wife sat with Desiree and Mr. Griddle.

The source of the shrieks was Mrs. Griddle clinging stubbornly to the deck rail.

"I won't get in, I won't! I'm not entrusting my life to that tinderbox!"

"Please get in, Mama," Desiree pleaded with her.

"I won't!" Mrs. Griddle's voice rose even higher.

"Then I will climb out and stay with you, Mama."

"You must not!" shouted out a voice from nowhere. "Let me deal with this."

Beard tugging in the wind and his hair dishevelled, Robert stepped up to Mrs. Griddle at the rail.

"Who are you?" she demanded. She peered closer and gave a screech. "I know you now! I know you!"

Robert seemed unperturbed that she had recognised him and without further ado he hoisted Mrs. Griddle over his shoulder and carried her over to the lifeboat, where he dumped her unceremoniously into the prow.

"How dare you, how dare you!" she spluttered.

Desiree clasped her mother closely, as two sailors signalled for the boat to be hauled over the side.

"Wait!" came Mr. Chandos's command.

Leonora, engrossed in the scene before her, had not been aware that he had returned to her side and that Finny was with him.

"I've been looking for you, miss!" panted Finny.

Before she could reply she found herself picked up in Mr. Chandos's arms and without pausing, he carried her over to the lifeboat and set her down gently.

She had told him she hated him and yet here he was taking infinite pains with her.

Mr. Chandos put a hand on Finny's shoulder.

"Go with Miss Cressy and take good care of her."

Finny nodded and leaped in beside Leonora.

Mr. Chandos signalled and the lifeboat lurched over the side to the sound of Mrs. Griddle saying her prayers.

It hit the surface and two crew immediately started rowing it away from the ailing *Teresa of the Sea*.

"I've got your shawl here, miss," whispered Finny.

Leonora scarcely felt the shawl as she was glued to the deck where figures ran to and fro. The second lifeboat was in the air and moving over the side.

Someone yelled from the deck and then clambered onto the rail.

It was Señor de Guarda. He balanced for a second, judging the distance between ship and swinging boat.

Then he leaped out. In mid-air he scrabbled for the edge of the lifeboat, missed it and went plunging on down into the fierce waves below.

Mrs. Griddle screamed.

The Señor's head bobbed up out of the water and he raised a despairing hand.

Leonora's hand went to her mouth as Mr. Chandos appeared at the rail.

One look over and he did not hesitate.

He stripped off his jacket, leaped onto the rail and dived into the sea in one bold move.

Leonora felt as if her heart had stopped beating as Mr. Chandos disappeared into the swell.

The lifeboat followed down fast and hit the surface with a crash throwing the passengers about.

Left of the lifeboat both Señor de Guarda and Mr. Chandos had surfaced, but the Señor seemed in a panic.

When Mr. Chandos reached for him, he caught hold so tightly that both went under. They rose again, gasping for air and then once again the waves swept over them and they were lost from view.

Leonora, watching breathlessly, fainted dead away.

Leonora opened her eyes.

She was lying on a couch in a room decorated with yellow walls and she was not alone. A maid in a white cap sat near an open French window.

"W-where am I?" she asked weakly.

"You are in the Governor's House on the Azores," said the maid. "You were brought ashore unconscious six hours ago – after the shipwreck."

She spoke the words carefully, but its effect was as she had obviously feared.

Leonora, with a cry of despair as she remembered all, leaped up and stumbled to the long window.

There was the sea and she frantically scanned its blue and unruffled surface.

"Where is the ship!" she moaned.

The maid bit her lip.

"Gone, miss."

Leonora pressed her hands to her face.

"Gone! And he is dead. Mr. Chandos is *dead*."

"No, all were saved. We sent out boats to help."

Leonora shook her head disbelievingly.

"No, no. I saw him – drown. I saw – two drown."

Troubled, the maid twisted her apron in her hand.

"Shall I send for some tea, miss?"

"No. Excuse me. I must – still be in shock."

"Well, if you'll excuse me miss, I was asked to help with the supper. There are so many extra guests now, as all the people from the ship are invited."

"Where are they staying?" asked Leonora, glad for a moment to believe that at least Finny and Desiree and all the others were safe.

"Some here and some at Admiral Broughton's."

"Broughton?"

"Yes. His niece Maud is staying with him. She's from England too, miss, like you. Well I must go, miss. The Governor's wife said she would call in on you later to bring you a choice of skirts."

Leonora glanced down, remembering that she was only clad in her white petticoat.

"I – look forward to meeting her," she said faintly.

The maid then left her and the tears burst forth from Leonora. She would never have believed it possible to feel so utterly wretched.

She had loved a man, then hated him, then lost him.

Only now did she really understand that love and hate were often one and the same.

She paced the room as if to escape the weight that had gathered in her breast. She could not. Her heavy heart went with her from corner to corner.

And now she contemplated how she would have to encounter Maud Broughton, whose face and voice would conjure up such vivid memories.

She became suddenly aware of the room darkening, and turned again towards the window.

She was astonished to see that the sun was sinking on the horizon as fast as a stone dropped into a pool.

Servants appeared with paper lanterns, which they began to hang from various trees.

Soon the garden looked so inviting that she stepped over the low sill and out, as she shook off her slippers and ran down to the edge of the garden where she could stare at the darkening sea.

"It's quite a sight, is it not, Miss Cressy?"

Leonora whirled round with a cry.

That voice – that oh, so familiar voice – had come from the shadow of the trees.

She scanned them with pounding heart.

Had she heard the voice of a ghost?

The figure of a man stepped out, a mere silhouette.

Was he real or a figment of desperate imagination?

"My sincere apologies, Miss Cressy, I do appear to have alarmed you. It is Lord Merton."

She flew at him, without thought, without caution. Flew at him and hammered his breast with her fists.

"You are dead. I saw you drown. You are *dead*."

Catching at her wrists, he gave a wry laugh.

"You may wish I was dead, Miss Cressy, but as you can see – as your fists can feel – I am not."

He let go and she fell back, panting, her eyes wild.

"And Señor de Guarda? I saw him drown too."

Lord Merton shook his head.

"I can assure you he is equally alive and well. The professor's sons dragged us both out of the water – at no little risk to themselves, for we were not a light haul!"

It seemed more than Leonora could bear – to have suffered such grief and then see Lord Merton so seemingly nonchalant before her.

She turned away to hide her tears.

"I see you are relieved that the Señor has survived, at any rate," he observed dryly.

"Certainly I am," replied Leonora, not untruthfully.

Troublesome as the Señor had been, she would not have wished him harm. She wiped her eyes quickly and turned back to find Lord Merton watching her closely.

"I heard – you were unconscious for some time."

"Oh, yes," she answered as gaily as she could. "It's a habit of mine, you know."

Her tone obviously puzzled Lord Merton, for there was a long pause.

Then suddenly he grasped her hand tightly.

"Come," he commanded.

Before she could make a protest she found herself half dragged across the lawn towards a stone bench that stood facing the bay below.

Here he took hold of her shoulders and forced her down.

"Let me go," she cried, struggling up. "I have no wish to stay any longer with Mr. Chandos or Lord Merton or – or whoever you are."

"Whoever I am?" he laughed. "It is precisely to clear up that matter that I wish you to stay."

Intrigued, she hesitated and then sank back down.

With a sigh he seated himself beside her.

"I was well aware of your existence long before I met you, Miss Cressy."

"H-how?"

"My parents emigrated to Brazil when I was young, but they never lost contact with the family in England. My mother's sister-in-law wrote to us regularly and mentioned you. Her name was Cressy – Doris Cressy."

Leonora gaped.

"Then you are *that* Arthur – Aunt Doris's nephew by marriage?"

"I am."

"Then that little dog – the chiahuahua was a present for her! But why did you not introduce yourself when I gave my name to your maid?"

Lord Merton gave a tight smile.

"You were too angry to give me the opportunity!"

Leonora had to admit that this was indeed the case.

"But," she persisted, "why did you not reply to my letter of condolence after my aunt died?"

Lord Merton drew in his breath.

"Because I had another reason for visiting England besides your aunt and, as I discovered, you were implicated in that reason in such a way that made a direct encounter between us difficult."

"What do you – mean?"

Lord Merton clenched his jaw.

"I had a partner in Brazil. He became ill and felt he should protect the prospects of his daughter in England by appointing a Guardian for her, a Mr. Farthing. This was a grave error for, when my friend died, Mr. Farthing left my friend's daughter without a penny. He stole her Trust fund and then disappeared."

"W-what was your – friend's name?"

"Lyford and his daughter is called Edith."

Leonora stared.

Edith Lyford, who had sobbed so when she had to leave Fenfold School!

"But why should the fact that I knew Edith – have made contact between you and I impossible?" she asked.

Lord Merton looked grave.

"When I heard what had befallen my good friend's daughter, I determined to bring this Mr. Farthing to justice. I hired a detective and soon discovered that Mr. Farthing had remarried under an assumed name."

Leonora held her breath.

"And that name was – ?"

"*Schilling*. He had changed his name to Schilling."

Leonora began to tremble.

"My – stepfather!"

Lord Merton nodded.

"When I heard you call yourself 'Cressy' that day outside the inn, I immediately guessed who you were and determined to be acquainted with you when the time was right. Then I arrived at Doris's and learned that her sister, your mother, had married a new husband – a Mr. Schilling!

"So imagine my severe predicament. You were the stepdaughter of the very man I sought to bring to justice. I had no idea of how to proceed, at least till I knew whether your mother and you were happy with the new connection. I decided to bide my time and find out more."

"So – when you came to Broughton Hall – it was to spy on Mr. Schilling?" ventured Leonora hopefully.

Lord Merton threw her a quick glance.

"That was one reason – yes."

'No doubt the other reason was Maud Broughton,' thought Leonora glumly. 'Probably Lord Merton's entire courtship of herself was merely a device to enable him to entrap Mr. Schilling.'

"Why didn't my stepfather realise who you were?"

"Because in his letters to Mr. Farthing, my partner, Lyford, would have referred to me as Mr. Chandos. I had only recently become Lord Merton, when a distant relative died and bequeathed me his title and estate. It was as Lord Merton that I first introduced myself to your stepfather."

Leonora tried to suppress a note of bitterness.

"Yes, at that notorious Club in Bristol. Where you tried to – *purchase* me! Like a horse at a country fair."

He regarded her closely, a twinkle in his eye.

"Forgive me. In the wild country I come from, it is quite natural to buy your bride."

"But why – *me*?"

Lord Merton looked away.

"When you revealed that you never wished to use the name of your stepfather, I knew that you hated him as much as I did and I realised then that you and your mother would welcome deliverance from him.

"But I needed to proceed with caution. I wanted to protect you and your mother from the ignominy attendant on being the wife and stepdaughter of a villain. I felt that the best way to do that would be to give you the protection of marriage."

Leonora reddened.

"You mean – you proposed to me out of charity?"

Lord Merton drew in his breath.

"By Heaven, but you make it difficult for a man!"

"On what basis should it be made so easy?" asked Leonora haughtily. "After all you seemed to be very much attached to Maud Broughton at the ball!"

"Maud Broughton? Who even now is pouring out her attentions on your erstwhile suitor, Señor de Guarda!"

"She – she is?"

He looked sidelong at her.

"If you wish to retain his interest," he said bitterly, "as it seemed you so often did on board ship, then you had better make haste. However, her fortune may prove more attractive to him than your beauty!"

"I never for one moment desired the attentions of Señor de Guarda! It's just that he found out I had stolen money from my stepfather and threatened to – reveal this to everyone unless I – humoured him."

"Ah! So that was it."

Leonora gave an involuntary shudder.

"I wonder what has become of him? Mr. Schilling, I mean."

"I can tell you. The moment I discovered you had fled, and why, I then made my move. Before setting off in pursuit I sent a message to the authorities and they came to arrest Mr. Schilling the same day.

"Do you recall the telegram I received on board? It informed me that your stepfather when attempting to evade arrest had fallen from a window and broken his neck!"

Leonora's hand flew to her mouth.

"*He is dead*?"

"He is dead," Lord Merton assured her solemnly.

"Then Mama is free! And I am free!"

Lord Merton's jaw clenched.

"You are indeed free, and I now no longer have the opportunity to offer you an escape from his clutches."

Leonora could not help her tart response.

"Oh, yes, indeed. Escape! As your *charity* bride!"

Lord Merton swung round.

His eyes blazed as she shrank back in alarm, almost expecting a blow, but the next instant his arm was around her waist and she was drawn towards him.

With a groan his lips met hers.

She struggled but for a moment.

His kiss was so insistent and his grip so powerful, her will melted.

With a soft cry she yielded.

As they became consumed in each other, an almost brutal intensity overcame them.

When at last he relinquished his hold, she fell back gasping.

"You fool – you fool," he murmured. "Don't you realise how I feel? In every letter your aunt wrote to my mother – and later to me – she extolled your virtues. She spoke of your beauty, your grace, your enquiring mind. I fell in love with you from a distance. And I think that was *exactly* what your aunt intended."

Leonora felt herself reeling.

"You – do?"

"Yes. She hinted as much before she died. She did not put you in her will because she expected *me* to provide for you. Would you accept that from me, Leonora?"

"I d-don't know. I still don't understand why you didn't tell me who you were – once we were on board ship. Why did you allow me to think you were just Mr. Chandos – and not Lord Merton as well?"

Lord Merton smiled.

"My dearest sweet darling, you were so determined never to entertain the suit of Lord Merton, I thought I had more chance to win you as Mr. Chandos!

"It was a very easy deceit to maintain because I had inherited my title so recently that the Captain and crew on my ship still thought of me by my old name. And when I encountered Finny at the Bristol docks and realised who he was, I took care to introduce myself as Chandos.

"Even so I asked him not to reveal who had helped him because I wanted *you* to entertain no preconceptions about the character of Mr. Chandos when you met him. I had suffered that disadvantage too much as Lord Merton!"

"So – nobody knew you as Lord Merton – not even Desiree!"

"Not even Desiree!"

Leonora sighed dreamily against his breast.

"Poor Desiree. I just wonder how Mrs. Griddle has behaved now that she knows Desiree's fiancé was on the ship all along."

"She has accepted the inevitable perhaps with some admiration for his persistence. She has now agreed to their being married."

"I am happy for them and even for Maud and Señor de Guarda if – if that too should prove a match!"

Lord Merton held her away from him.

"So am I. But oh, what terrible jealousy I suffered when I believed that you favoured that man! Swear to me, swear to me that he is not still in your heart."

Leonora trembled.

"I could never have cared for him. *Never*! But tell me when I first met you as Mr. Chandos on board ship, you said I reminded you of 'someone dear?' Who was that?"

"You cannot guess? It was *you* – the you I held in my arms at Broughton Hall, my darling."

Leonora looked at him with relief.

"I am glad you were not thinking of another love."

Lord Merton scanned her face, his eyes burning.

"You are my *only* love. So my treasure, humour me! Indulge me! Let me hear my name on your lips."

Leonora twinkled shyly.

"Which one?"

Lord Merton threw back his head with a roar.

"I deserved that!"

The next moment he drew her against him again and buried his lips in her hair.

"Perhaps you would deign to call me by another name entirely, my dearest one."

Leonora, her flesh alive under his touch, swooned.

"What is that?"

"*Husband*," came his soft reply.

She pulled away and stared at him, startled.

"H-husband?"

"Husband. Will you marry me, Leonora?"

She answered him "*yes*" with a loud cry and their lips met again with increased fervour.

Her blood pulsed and her flesh seemed to burn.

All that held her was his strength, for her body was weak with desire.

There was no more reason to hide from love.

She was his, only his, until the very end of time.